KT-148-179

HEATWAVE

HEATWAVE

A novel

VICTOR JESTIN

Translated from the French by Sam Taylor

SCRIBNER

LONDON NEW YORK SYDNEY TORONTO NEW DELHI

First published in the United States by Scribner,
an imprint of Simon & Schuster, Inc., 2021
First published in Great Britain by Scribner,
an imprint of Simon & Schuster UK Ltd, 2021

Copyright © 2019 by Flammarion

English language translation copyright © 2021 by Sam Taylor
Originally published in France in 2019 by Flammarion as *La chaleur*

The right of Flammarion to be identified as the author of
this work has been asserted in accordance with the
Copyright, Designs and Patents Act, 1988.

SCRIBNER and design are registered trademarks of The Gale Group, Inc.,
used under licence by Simon & Schuster Inc.

1 3 5 7 9 10 8 6 4 2

Simon & Schuster UK Ltd
1st Floor
222 Gray's Inn Road
London WC1X 8HB

www.simonandschuster.co.uk
www.simonandschuster.com.au
www.simonandschuster.co.in

Simon & Schuster Australia, Sydney
Simon & Schuster India, New Delhi

A CIP catalogue record for this book is available from the British Library

Hardback ISBN: 978-1-4711-9977-6
eBook ISBN: 978-1-4711-9978-3
eAudio ISBN: 978-1-3985-0168-3

Interior design by Wendy Blum
Printed in the UK by CPI Group (UK) Ltd, Croydon, CR0 4YY

"You're running around like an open razor blade.
You might cut someone."

—Georg Büchner, from *Woyzeck*, translated by Henry J. Schmidt

Oscar is dead because I watched him die and did nothing. He was strangled by the ropes of a swing, like one of those children you read about in newspapers. But Oscar was not a child. At seventeen, you don't die like that by accident. You tie the rope around your neck because you want to feel something. Maybe he was trying to find a new form of pleasure. After all, that was what we were here for: the pleasure. Anyway, I did nothing. Everything stemmed from that.

IT WAS THE last Friday in August. Late at night; the campsite was sleeping. The only ones still up were the teenagers on the beach. I was seventeen, too, but I wasn't with them. I was trying to sleep, and their music was keeping me awake. It reached me from the dune, along with the sounds of the waves and their laughter. When it stopped, I could hear my parents moving around in their tent. I was restless. I could feel stones under my inflatable mattress. The sand stuck to my skin. Sometimes I would start to fall asleep and then someone on the beach would yell. It was a sort of fierce joy directed against me, a wild, pulsing dance around my tent. I was exhausted. One more day and the vacation would be over.

That night I decided to get up and go for a walk outside. All was calm on this side of the dune. The tents and the bungalows were lost in shadows. The only light came from the condom vending machine. "Protect yourself," it said. Though what it really meant was: *Do it.* Every night, proud and ashamed, the teenagers would buy some. Buying a condom was already like doing it a little bit. Often it would end up as a balloon, burst in the air, like a dying hope. I knew all the colors of that campsite. For two weeks I'd been roaming its paths aimlessly, killing time. I'd gone to all the parties. I'd made an effort. And every night, after a few drinks, I'd walked away, pretending to go to the bar for another beer, then walking along the shore and returning unseen to my tent. But I hardly slept. The music didn't stop. I felt like there was something lodged in my chest that kept me up until dawn.

It was while wandering aimlessly that night that I came upon Oscar. I walked past the playground and saw him on the swing. He was drunk. The ropes were coiled around his neck. First I wondered what he was doing there. I'd seen him earlier, dancing on the beach with the others.

I'd seen him kiss Luce and I'd almost vomited, I remember; their bodies, practically naked, had stood out in the darkness. I watched him alone on the swing and I realized he was dying. The ropes were slowly strangling him. He had done that on his own and, to judge from the expression on his face, he might have changed his mind. I didn't move. Nothing moved on that secluded playground. The moon was hidden behind the tall pine trees. Suddenly Oscar saw me: his eyes met mine and they didn't let go. He opened his mouth, but no sound came out. He kicked his feet, but his body hung still. We looked at each other like that. It was true that I'd sometimes wished he would die, certain days, seeing him smile in his blue trunks. On the other side of the dune, the music kept playing. I recognized the chorus: *Blow a kiss, fire a gun . . . We need someone to lean on* . . . It took a long time. Strangulation is not a quick way of dying. The moment of his death was drawn out and I didn't notice when it happened. I just felt more and more alone. After a while his head fell forward, propelling the ropes in the other direction. They started unwinding, faster and faster, until finally they released him. His body slumped lifeless onto the rubberized floor of the playground.

I hadn't made many stupid mistakes in my seventeen years of life. This one was difficult to understand. It all happened too fast; I felt powerless. I walked up to Oscar and touched his shoulder. I shook him. I hit him. His vacant stare passed over me when I moved his body. I wanted to think, but then I heard sounds coming from the beach. A small group headed toward the campsite. They were talking in loud voices. They were drunk, too. I thought they'd be able to hear me. I called out, but my voice didn't carry far; it stayed close to me. The others walked away, laughing. "Shut up!" a man shouted from his tent. They disappeared. On the beach, the music stopped. The last teenagers passed by. I remained standing there, on the playground, making no attempt to hide. No one saw me. At last I was absolutely alone, with Oscar, who continued being dead at my feet.

Suddenly it occurred to me that I'd killed him, and this thought crowded out all the others. There was nothing left but his heavy body. And then I had a very clear memory of a large hole that some children had dug in the dune that afternoon. It seemed obvious to me that Oscar had to disappear. I didn't give it any further thought. I did think that maybe this was the stupidest mistake of all, but I did it anyway, just to do something. I grabbed his legs. He wasn't that heavy. I dragged him. We advanced slowly, first through the playground and then along a gravel path, across some grass, some sand. The weight of the body varied according to the surface. I concentrated on my movements so I wouldn't have to think about anything else, wouldn't understand the significance of those moments. I was just dragging a body, that was all. I took a break in front of the dune. All was calm. Oscar was very calm. The air was cooler now, almost pleasant. It must have been the middle of the night. We climbed even more slowly, sinking into the sand, getting caught on thistles. Many people hurt themselves here, running barefoot. Finally the beach appeared. It was deserted, the sand strewn with trash that would have to be cleaned up the next morning. I thought about leaving Oscar in the water and letting the backwash take him. But the tide was too low. The sea was a long way off and I was already out of breath. I decided to stick with the hole. I left Oscar where he was, walked around the dune, and found it easily, near the lifeguard's flag. It was too small. I crouched down and made it big enough to fit a teenage boy. I didn't like the feel of the sand under my fingernails or the rasp it made when I scooped it up, but I forced myself to keep digging anyway. When I was satisfied, I went back to fetch Oscar. I dragged him to the hole and pushed him in, his legs folded to the side. His face was dirty, covered with dust. I wiped it off with my fingertips. Then I threw sand over it, and all over his body, too. This took a long time. I didn't think about anything. I listened to the waves and the sound of my breathing.

At last the hole was just sand, and Oscar, underground, weighed less heavy. He even disappeared a little. I stood up and looked at the clear sky. Music rose quietly into the air. I realized that the sound was coming from under the sand. I got down on my knees and dug, undoing all my work. He was well buried. The music kept playing, on a loop. At last I reached Oscar—his cell phone was ringing inside his swimming trunks: *Luce calling*. I turned it off and stuffed it into my pocket. Nobody had heard it. There weren't any people nearby. I caught my breath and filled in the hole again, just as carefully as I had the first time.

It must have been very late. I was alone and everything seemed in its right place. The beach and the campsite, on either side of the dune, were silent under the stars. I wanted to do something again. On all fours, like a dog, I retraced my path and erased my footsteps. When that was done, I still didn't dare go back to my tent. I thought about my parents, who were sleeping now, about my sister and my brother, also sleeping. All the parties were over. I decided to go for a walk on the beach. I went along the shore, my feet in the water. The low tide revealed rocks I had never seen before. Little by little, I felt as if my body were going numb, bruised by my exertions. I tried to think about what I'd done and to feel something. But my eyelids were heavy. I staggered toward the sea. The sky was starting to lighten.

I went back to the campsite. On the way, I passed a jogger who went into the forest. Inside my tent, I fell asleep fully clothed. I was about to live through the last day—and the hottest day—of my vacation. In fact, it was the hottest day the country had known in seventeen years. That was what the forecast had said. They'd made the announcement through the loudspeakers attached to the pine trees, one of which was just above my tent. It woke me every morning.

◆

"WELL, HELLOOOO CAMPERS! This is your pink bunny! It's Saturday already! Many of you will be leaving us this weekend, so make the most of your last day. Have fun! Be happy! As for me, I'll see you all in thirty minutes at the pool for water aerobics!"

I opened my eyes, already furious. It was eight o'clock, and inside the tent, the heat was becoming unbearable. The sun beat down on the canvas, forcing us outside, where it could really get to work on us. But the campers were happy. Sometimes they complained, they collapsed with exhaustion, their skin flaked and peeled, but they were still happy, still believed that summer was the best season of all.

Suddenly everything spiraled. My body tensed and I saw Oscar again: the playground, the hole. I didn't move. I stared vacantly at a stain on the canvas and tried to imagine the dune in broad daylight, people running and laughing, kites flying. I couldn't hear anyone outside. My family and my dog were in Dax, the nearest town, and would not return until lunch. I remembered that now. I was alone. It was my lucky morning, when I could sleep until noon, gaining half a day without my parents forcing me to make the most of it. But I got up. I took a few steps outside the tent. My parents had left a bowl of cereal for me on the folding table. Our colorful towels hung from the line that my father had tied between two pines. I didn't see the point of this: they were dry within seconds anyway. I left our camping spot. As soon as I was past the first hedge, I started running—straight to the dune.

The campsite was waking up, the machine juddering to life. Heads poked out of tents. Children ran along sunbaked paths, and their mothers' arms caught them, plastering them with sunscreen to make sure they didn't burn. Old people met at intersections without a word and walked to the pétanque courts, just as they did every morning of every day of their vacation. A flood of campers poured toward the beach. It was a well-known campsite in the Landes, in the southwest corner of France. Three stars. Surrounded by pine forest. Close to the ocean. Swimming pool with slide. Children's playground. Karaoke, gym, special events every night. There were lots of teenagers who were there for the partying; there were large families, old Dutch couples, kids learning to surf. Dogs were allowed.

I climbed the dune. The sand burned my feet. I wasn't wearing my flip-flops; I must have lost them, here, last night . . . I tried to remember. It wasn't the same place anymore, with the colors and the smiles. It was all too bright, too cheerful, for someone to be dead. As long as I didn't see the hole, the hole did not exist. But I found it quickly, and instantly I saw myself dragging, digging, burying, like a shadow among the happy campers running down to the beach. It was there, in the middle of the dune, a hole filled in, with Oscar at the bottom. For me, it was a hole filled in. For the others, it was just sand, a hole filled in with sand among all the other filled-in holes of the majestic sand dune, the campsite's pride and glory. The lifeguard's flag stood next to it like a marker. Children ran over, walked on, trampled Oscar.

To start with, I panicked. I paced around the hole. Like a dog, I stared at the people who approached it, and they looked at me as if I were crazy. Did I have sunstroke at nine in the morning? It wasn't *that* hot, surely. It would be unbearable by noon. Everything would start to bake. I calmed down. Forced myself to think. Oscar had strangled himself with the ropes of a swing and he was dead. I had to tell them that. It was an accident. I had to call the police or an ambulance. But I didn't remember the phone numbers. I was tired. I was numb. I wanted to sleep. And then I felt something that made me aware of my body again: a small rectangle of pressure against my thigh. It was Oscar's phone, in the pocket of my trunks. I remembered now: the music in the night. I took it out. I saw my reflection in the black screen: dirty face, greasy hair, eyes puffy from the tears I wasn't crying because I hadn't understood yet, because I was still Leonard, so shy and nice, who didn't like the heat and preferred gray days.

Louis came along and patted my shoulder. I smiled at him, an old reflex of politeness, my first smile of the day, twisting my lips into an unnatural shape.

"Hey, Leo, how's it going? Coming for a swim? I'm going to meet this girl. You should see the ass on her . . ."

◆

THE BEACH WAS already packed. Sun umbrellas, games of paddleball, people swimming . . . it was a hive of continual activity, a factory running at full power. The bodies piled up on the strip of sand and overflowed into the sea, swarmed, advanced, and gradually scattered into distant swimmers, surfers, floating heads, and stray yellow buoys. Sitting on the sand, I listened to the waves. I was beginning to understand what I had done. Nobody suspected me. Nobody even looked at me. I just seemed ill at ease. I'd always been a nervous boy, and now I was even more on edge; on the surface, that was the only change caused by Oscar's death.

"What's up with you? Are you sulking?"

"No."

"What happened to you last night? I didn't see you leave."

"I was tired. I went back to my tent."

The sentences came out on their own, cold and terse. Louis didn't seem to mind. He didn't have any other friends, so he put up with me. He'd wrapped his T-shirt around his head like a turban, slathered his stocky body with sunscreen, pulled the legs of his shorts higher up his thighs. He was smiling the way he always did when he wanted to talk about girls. And I was annoyed with him—I was annoyed with everyone on the beach—for failing to hear my silent screams, for failing to guess.

"This fucking sun . . . You should cover your head."

"I'm okay."

"Well, she should be here soon. She's called Zoe. She looks nice in her photos, but who knows? She might be a real dog."

He showed me the photographs of Zoe from her Tinder profile. He had laughed at me on the first day because I'd never heard of it. He'd explained how the app worked: you chose a few photographs of yourself and wrote a paragraph about your likes and dislikes; the profiles of girls and boys in the area appeared on your phone; if you liked someone, you sent a message; if they liked you, too, you could have a conversation and get to know each other, even meet up in real life. "It's mostly for fucking, obviously, although there are always a few annoying girls who just want to chat, and some Korean girls on Erasmus or whatever who want you to take them to see the Eiffel Tower." The app's logo had a curious shape, halfway between an egg and a flame, and every time I'd wondered why, a small sharp panic had pinched my heart, so I preferred to keep my distance from it, just like I kept my distance from girls and dancing and all the other things that we were here for.

"Leo, listen. If I don't get laid today, I'm giving up

on the beach. I've had enough of this bullshit. HEY, GIRLS!"

I jumped. Zoe was arriving, with a friend.

"See, she hasn't come on her own . . . Hang on, who's that she's with? Luce? Do they know each other? That's funny."

They were laughing as they came toward us, because Luce had recognized us. I'd recognized her, too; the night before, Luce had been dancing with Oscar, and I'd watched her kiss him on the dune. She was wearing a red sarong. She stood out starkly against the sun.

"All right, back me up here," Louis said in my ear. "She likes you, too, you know."

They stood in front of us. "Hi." Zoe was smoking a cigarette, taking little puffs as if she were nauseated but trying not to show it.

Louis stood up to kiss them on the cheeks and make the introductions. "I'm Louis. And this is Leonard. So you know each other, Zoe and Luce? That's funny. Small world."

Zoe frowned. "This campsite is hardly the world."

"Figure of speech."

"Hungover, Leonard?" Luce asked.

I shook my head, smiling weakly. Louis clapped his hands. "I'm going to swim. You coming, Zoe?"

"Why not?"

He winked at me and they set off together.

Luce sat down next to me. "Were you on the beach, too, last night?"

"Yeah, but I went back early."

"How come? You didn't like the party?"

"Not that much."

I didn't dare turn to face her. I kept staring at the sea. I watched sailboats, a liner in the distance. Beyond that, the waves were wilder, higher. People were maybe drowning. Luce's hand brushed some sand off my knee. I thought I was going to faint. She couldn't see how pale I was because the sunlight made everything pale. Sometimes it revealed imperfections in the skin, sometimes it erased them, making the ugliest people more beautiful. I knew how to position myself to look my best. I still had that much pride. I'd had time to look carefully at the sky while the others were moving around below. Louis didn't do that. He let the sun expose his zits and the blond fluff on his upper lip. He never paid attention to the little things: after lunch, he didn't brush his teeth, and he smelled of fries; he didn't take a shower after swimming in the sea, either, so his skin stayed salty. He took none of the precautions that punctuated my days, and yet he was at ease in the water with a girl, and I watched him splashing in his joy as I lay there, motionless on the beach, with a vast emptiness inside my chest.

"What are you thinking about?" Luce asked.

"Nothing."

"I never see you around. Where's your tent?"

"Number three-thirty."

"Are you camping with Louis?"

"No."

"Who are you with, then?"

"My parents."

"You sound like you're ashamed of it."

"A bit."

"You shouldn't be. You're lucky. Where are you from?"

"Lorient."

"Don't know it. Are you a senior, too? What do you want to do after high school?"

"Musicology."

"Oh, you're a musician?"

"Yeah."

"That's cool. And you really love to chat, right?"

"What do you mean?"

"You're funny. Why don't you take off your T-shirt? You must be hot."

"I'm fine . . . thanks."

"Come on, let's go swimming."

She stood up. I refused politely. She didn't insist, just took off her sarong and ran to join the others, her feet seeming to bounce lightly on the sand. Her skin was pale; she didn't tan. She disappeared into the sea and I found myself alone in the crowd. The naked torsos of volleyball players sprang into the air. Swimmers threw themselves into the waves. Parents took their children away from the sea so they wouldn't die in the riptides. Louis and Zoe were already laughing. Luce dived into the crashing waves and reappeared each time somewhere else. Parts of her body glistened as the water moved over her. Suddenly I wanted to go with her. I stood up, but everything around me rose more slowly, as if I'd been drinking. A man walked past with a metal detector. A child screamed in a wave. I twisted my neck and saw the flag, the hole, Oscar's body. What the hell am I doing here, I thought, and the feeling was stronger than it had been on the other days. I left the beach and walked over the dune. I didn't say goodbye. They didn't see me leave anyway.

◆

ON THE OTHER side was the same strange world. The heat was rising, the sunlight pouring down on the paths. Some madman was grilling sausages like it was noon already. Music blared from the loudspeakers: "Top Summer Hits." Twenty-five songs. I'd noticed it on the first day: the same twenty-five songs were played on a permanent loop, like at a supermarket. Not loud enough to disturb anyone but loud enough that the music insinuated itself everywhere, like the sun, the sand, and the water of the Landes: *If you go hard you gotta get on the floor . . . If you're a party freak then step on the floor . . .* All around, people were enjoying their vacation. They didn't want to hear me. Besides, I had nothing to say. I could say: Oscar is dead. But I didn't even believe it. I tried to think about him, and I could do it only in fits and starts. I could feel his phone burning against my thigh. I could have taken it to the lost property office. But it was a long way. I'd have had to cross the whole campsite, then line up at the reception desk with all the sunburned campers, the lost children, the new arrivals, and the foreigners who didn't understand anything; I'd have had to wait as the multilingual receptionist was called so that she could explain to them in English, German, Spanish, or Flemish the rules of the campsite and the hours of the water aerobics class, before attaching a little blue bracelet to everyone's wrist, uniting us all for eternity. I'd managed to cut mine off with a steak knife on the first day.

I collapsed onto a bench. I needed my parents. Maybe I'd be able to tell them. But they probably weren't back yet. I had no idea what time it was.

I looked around and recognized the playground from the night before. The swing was there with its spotless ropes. Where had I stood to watch Oscar die? I couldn't remember. I felt like I was looking at another playground, a movie set that had been placed there. Children were playing. Most of them were spinning around endlessly on a merry-go-round in the shape of a crocodile.

"It's not a crocodile, it's an alligator," a girl said to a boy. "A crocodile has a pointy mouth, and an alligator has a round mouth, so this is an alligator."

She stared proudly at the boy and he shook his head.

I examined the alligator, its yellow eyes, its green shell, the metal bar that came out of its mouth so that the children could hang on to it. I felt my lip tremble and tears rise up, like people arriving late for a party. I had not made many stupid mistakes in seventeen years. And nothing *really* stupid. I'd never cheated, stolen, punched anyone. Only rarely had I insulted anyone. I had accumulated my hate and anger slowly, patiently. It wasn't an accident. I had let Oscar die. I could have saved him and I hadn't. And then I'd hidden his body. I couldn't remember why. I could have just walked away. They'd have found him where he died. They'd have seen the marks on his neck, they'd have measured the alcohol in his bloodstream, they'd have noted the time of his death. A cold wave would have crashed down on everyone in the campsite and they'd all have gone far away from here, me included. But I'd buried him. That was the *really* stupid mistake. I'd spent the whole night burying a body.

I turned on his phone. I didn't know the code. I knew nothing about him. All I had was this locked screen with a photograph of a mountain and two missed calls, one from Luce, one from his mother. I remembered his mother. I'd seen her a few times on the beach. People had made fun of Oscar because he was camping with her. Every night she would walk back alone to her bungalow. I remembered the bungalow, too. I could go and look for it; Oscar's blue towel would be hanging on the guardrail, much too dry by now. I could find his mother and talk to her. She would listen to me.

I started walking toward the bungalows. On the way, I felt my vision blurring, the ground softening. For two weeks I had wandered around this campsite, fleeing the sun, sticking to the shadows cast by trees and tents, killing time. But I didn't bother with that now. I walked bareheaded in the light. A pleasant numbness enveloped me, preventing me from thinking too far ahead. At the end of a path, I thought I recognized Oscar's bungalow. The deck was empty, the door open. No one ever closed anything at the campsite. Everyone trusted everyone else. I went over. I climbed the three little steps. A fan stirred the hammock hanging in a corner. There was no one around. A bodyboard covered with sand. Some empty rosé bottles. My vision grew more blurred. Someone was moving around inside. It all happened calmly: I staggered, Oscar's mother came out, she caught my arm and helped me into the hammock. I let myself be rocked in the gentle breeze from the fan. She brought me a glass of water and sat facing me.

"Feeling better? It's a hundred and two degrees and it's supposed to keep getting hotter. Are you friends with Oscar?"

I couldn't answer. I had come to tell her everything, but I didn't know how to begin. Just opening my mouth was difficult. So I looked at her—I stared into her eyes like I'd stared into Oscar's—and I thought about the fact that she was his mother so the nausea would force the words out.

She turned away. Leaning on the guardrail, she lit a cigarette. Her dress showed a constellation tattooed on her bare
back. She was the kind of person my parents looked down
on a little bit.

"What's your name?"

"Leonard."

"I'm Claire."

Claire. I realized I would never tell her anything.

"You're really out of it, aren't you? You should rest. I
don't know where Oscar is—he didn't sleep here last night.
Do you want to wait for him here?"

I shrugged. This amused her.

"So what do you think of this campsite?"

"It's okay . . ."

"You're not drinking too much at night?"

"No."

"Are you here with friends? With your parents? Do you
think it's really horrible, camping with your mother? Is it
embarrassing with girls?"

"No . . ."

"You should tell Oscar that."

She turned around to smile at me. Oscar wasn't that
good-looking; I remembered his face. He could appear
quite handsome from a distance, in the sun, but his features
were heavy, and his eyes always looked tired.

"These are the best years of your life, you know—you
should make the most of them. We're leaving this after-

noon. We'll come back next summer, but we'll bring a tent. The bungalows are kind of a rip-off."

She smiled at me again and I lowered my head so I couldn't see her anymore, and also so that she'd question me, shake me, discover the truth herself, since I couldn't talk or cry and I looked like butter wouldn't melt in my mouth. I sensed her moving away behind me. She went inside. I was alone again, in the immense silence.

My head tilted the landscape. A conga line was going past. The pink bunny was leading some teenagers toward the beach. They were singing. Sometimes their arms lifted and seemed to point to the sun. They weren't suffering. The heat had been rising for the past few summers. Every year, it got hot earlier—this year it had been in February—and we had welcomed it without fear, happy to see the end of winter; we'd sat out on café terraces with no sense of foreboding about what it might mean. We didn't sense the inferno coming. I wondered what temperature would finally be too hot. Everything would flip then. People would flee the campsite like it was a house on fire and the bunny would be left to dance alone. I wanted to move. I hated myself for just lying there doing nothing. But my eyes were closing. Sleep was taking me at last. Nobody ever slept much here. We went to bed late and got up with the rising sun to march side by side with the others, toward joy.

♦

"FOLLOWING AN INCIDENT on the beach, we ask you to keep your dogs tied up in the shade . . . In fact, you should all get in the shade, too. It's a hundred and four degrees out there, guys!"

Luce came toward me in her red sarong. I was dozing. I thought: She's found me. I shrank into the hammock so she wouldn't see me.

Claire came out. "Are you looking for Oscar?"

"Yes!"

"Are you his girlfriend?"

"Not really."

"I don't know where he is . . . But I've got another one here, if you're interested. He's sleeping . . ."

I sat up, embarrassed. Luce did not look surprised. She came toward me, hands behind her back, and pretended to look me over.

"Yeah . . . He'll do . . . What's his name?"

"Leonard. He doesn't say much, but he's nice."

"Is it normal that he's all red like that?"

They laughed together. I thought they were cruel. Luce winked at me. I winked back without thinking.

"I'm going to the pool. Aren't you hot?" she asked.

I got out of the hammock and stood in front of her. I had never looked at her this closely before. She was quite tall, with brown eyes. Freckles full of sunlight.

"Come on, Leonard."

I felt flattered. I followed her, like a little dog. I walked past Claire, and for a moment, I almost spoke. I opened my mouth, then closed it again.

She laughed. "Go on, go with her. What are you waiting for?"

The campsite had its own laws. Two weeks of vacation was a lifetime. We arrived like newborns, pale and alone. We left with a sigh of sadness or relief, like the dying. Friendships were made and unmade in the time it took to walk down a path. Hearts were lost and broken in a single day. A few times I'd seen Luce and Oscar being friends, being in love, or ignoring each other. Now I was walking with her as if I were him. Some boys watched us. She waved at the ones she knew. Her sarong brushed against my hand as we walked.

"I didn't realize you knew Oscar's mother."

"I don't know her."

"But you were in her hammock."

"Yeah."

She smiled. She thought I was funny, and more intelligent than I actually was. This often happened: in my embarrassment, I would say absurd things, and everyone would think I was really witty and deep.

"Do you get along well with Oscar?"

"I don't know."

"Why did you leave without saying goodbye before?"

"I didn't feel too good. Sorry."

At worst, I looked like I was sulking. I gripped the

phone in my pocket. My trunks were making me itch. My thoughts and the heat combined to create rivers of sweat on my skin, but I just looked like a spoiled little brat.

"Why are you making that face?"

"This is how I always look."

She accepted my answers. I could stand her more easily than the others. Something was different with her. But all the same, I wanted to leave. My parents must be back by now.

"I have to go eat lunch."

"Already? Meet me at the pool after!"

I turned onto a different path. Behind me, I heard her say:

"You know, Oscar's really not my boyfriend. We're just close."

◆

MY FATHER WAS making lunch. My mother was reading a thriller. Alma was riding around them on her tricycle, and Bubble, our dog, a beautiful Newfoundland, was sleeping in the shade of a hedge. Seeing all those familiar faces, I felt suddenly calm, and a wave of love and courage rose up within me: they would hear me. When my father saw me, he threw a round cheese at me.

"Good catch! We pillaged the market in Dax! I was like, *Can I have a taste?* And they gave me a piece of cheese! *Can I taste?* Yup, another piece of cheese! I bought one in the end. I'd have felt guilty otherwise. So how are you?"

"Sit down," said my mother, pushing a plate in front of me. "We were calling you. Don't you have your phone?"

I shook my head. Alma stared at me. "You're all red."

"Where's Adrien?" I asked suddenly.

"He's with his surf buddies."

"We gave him his freedom . . . It's okay, at fifteen, don't you think?"

At my feet, Bubble was panting. He couldn't sleep in this heat: his tongue lolled and he looked sad. He was hotter than all of us put together. He couldn't go bare-chested. Then again, neither could I.

"Bubble's too hot. He got aggressive this morning. You should watch out . . ."

"Apparently a dog went mad earlier on the beach. It bit a child."

"Will it bite me, too?"

"No, sweetie."

"Are you protecting yourself, Leo?"

"Yes."

"I mean, are you wearing sunscreen?"

"Yes."

"We won't be leaving until late this afternoon. No rush. You have time to enjoy yourself."

The tabbouleh, still in its packaging, was surrounded by mustard-flavored chips. Some cherry tomatoes were arranged on top of a green salad in the shape of a smiling face. My father leaned close to me. "So . . . did you go out last night?"

"Yes."

"We could hear your music from here. We went to karaoke. That was good, too. There was this guy in a bunny suit. He wanted to tie a carrot to my belt so I'd try to get it into a bottle by moving my hips . . . You get the idea. I refused, obviously."

"I'm sorry . . . I'm not hungry." I pushed the plate away and stood up.

"Got a hot date?"

"Stop it," my mother hissed.

"Oh, come on, I'm allowed to ask!"

"You don't have to answer, Leo."

"Is she pretty, at least?"

My mother shot him a look to make him shut up. I was just as embarrassed by her prudishness. There was a silence. They could tell that something was wrong. It was the moment to speak up. Adrien was with his surf friends. They could ask Alma to go and play. I'd say: Listen . . . But there was just that silence, the smell of the pines, Bubble's panting, and our last day at this three-star campsite. We usually spent our family vacations with my grandparents. But my parents had been looking forward to this trip since the fall. Some evenings, coming back from work, they had shown us photographs of the Landes and live video feeds so we could see the beach in every season. The preparations had taken a long time. First we'd had to buy tents, camping equipment, and bodyboards. Then we'd had to drive across France. We'd had to pay extra for a spot with a view and direct access to the beach. Finally, there had been the outings and the restaurants to take us to the limits of pleasure. They had often repeated that the landscape was beautiful—"so beautiful"—to help us fully appreciate it. Once, a gray cloud had appeared in the sky, and each of us, even Alma, had pretended not to see it so that nothing would spoil our joy. The sky had stayed blue. The heat had blown away the memory of months of rain. The vacation had been perfect. My parents had done everything they could to make it that way. I had seen them counting the days, regretting each evening that happiness flew by so quickly. I had counted the days, too. For two weeks, I had been waiting for their vacation to end. I couldn't ruin it even more by telling them about Oscar, his body buried, in such happy times. So I kept my mouth shut.

"Eat your salad, Leo, or you'll waste away."

"Shut up, Alma, I'm not in the mood. Anyway, it's not true."

◆

ADRIEN AND I had to take turns doing the dishes after each meal. He always complained when it was his turn, and afterward we ate from plates that were slightly dirty, because he'd been in a rush to get back to having fun. But when it was my turn, I did it without being asked. Everyone else ran to the beach while I got to work at the communal sinks. I couldn't swim or sunbathe or drink because I was too busy scrubbing. In the shadow of the restrooms, I slowly slid my hands into the soapy water. People walked past unsuspecting. They thought I was doing chores. For a long time I let my thoughts wander. Sometimes, as I stood by the sink, I would feel a moment of excitement, but it was always followed by sadness, because I had to admit that, deep down, buried inside me, was a secret desire to join the others, to dance. But I didn't move. I rubbed at the mayonnaise stains, wishing that they wouldn't disappear. And when there was really nothing left to do, I went back to the tent with the cleanest dishes in the world and a pair of damaged hands, the skin worn away after so much time spent working to avoid fun. My father always told me not to bother: we would eat from the same plates again anyway. I was wasting my time. This vacation was for me, too. I shouldn't let it be ruined by my obsessions.

I was in the middle of washing the dishes when Louis appeared behind me. He often seemed to bump into me: strange, at such a large campsite. He said: "It's funny how we always bump into each other." He was the only person to seek out my company. I didn't really care. He helped me take the plates back to the tent and he said hello to my parents. They exchanged a few words about the weather: It's hot, very hot, but we shouldn't complain, that's why we're here, etc. Then the two of us went to the shack at the beach where they sold fries. Louis wanted to eat. We walked alongside the hole. A dog was sniffing the sand. Seeing this, I wanted to chase it away: I was afraid that it would start digging, unearth the body, and that I'd be caught because of my fingerprints on Oscar's neck. Then for a moment I was afraid that the dog would never start digging; that I would be left, this summer and all the following summers, eternally trailing Louis as he went to buy fries and talk about sex.

"I'm not saying I have no chance with Zoe, but it's not a sure thing, either, so I should keep looking. But I don't have anyone else ... The problem with Tinder, in fact, is that you base your demands on what you think of yourself, if you see what I mean. For example, that girl over there, look ... I like her, but I'm sure she wouldn't like me, so I act as if I don't like her, either, when the truth is, I'd totally fuck her."

He was slumped in his deck chair, almost naked, with his shorts rolled up the tops of his thighs, sweating and panting. A bit like Bubble. His finger angrily swiped girls' profiles. On Tinder, you were limited to fifty profiles per day. After that, you had to pay. Louis paid. "Well, if I didn't spend it on this, I'd just spend it on something else. Fuck the capitalists—I'll buy what I like. It's my cash, I can do what I want with it!" Spending that money entitled him to all the girls on the application. He swiped them one by one, and with his lack of success came a new weariness in the movement of his finger. His swiping grew more mechanical, and he grew more tolerant. As always, he ended up accepting anyone who would have him.

"Fuck. That's it. There aren't any more."

I was only half-listening to him. I was sinking into a sort of trance. The colored patches of the sun umbrellas rippled like blurred reflections, as if someone had thrown a stone at the surface of the scene.

"Leo, did you hear what I said?"

"There aren't any more?" I repeated, eyes closed.

"No more chicks, right. 'There is no one around you. Please try later.' That means I've looked at every single profile on this campsite. That sucks, man!"

But there are people around us, I thought, sunbathing in deck chairs, playing paddleball, swimming in the sea; and a few others, alone, waiting . . .

"So what do I do now? Apart from Zoe, I don't have anyone . . . Maybe I could broaden the search zone, like a radius of six miles? Shit, but I'm not going all the way to Dax just to get laid . . ."

I sensed him slumping more deeply into his deck chair.

"Never mind. There's always Zoe. It's Zoe or nothing. She must be at her yoga thing. I'm going to go."

But he didn't go. He stayed where he was, macerating in the heat.

"It's partly my fault, too. Those three photos I chose are crap. I look stupid in them. Why am I going bare-chested when I'm fat? Look at this little fat belly . . . Why don't I keep my T-shirt on, like you? Huh? Leo, are you asleep?"

"What? I don't know."

"I should just jerk off—it's all the same in the end. It's true: I get all excited looking at Tinder, but I don't find anyone, and then I jerk off and everything's fine. I just nip the desire in the bud. All the same, it'd be shit if I never did it for real . . . I don't want to have to pay for prostitutes or do disgusting stuff. I mean, you could end up doing some really seedy shit if you're desperate, you could kill yourself . . ."

Suddenly he stood up and stared around at the other people with a crazed look on his face. "I want to fuck! WHOA!"

"Shut your mouth," said the guy selling fries.

Louis sat down, snickering. He was sweating a lot. His laughter gradually died away and he started drowsing. His phone lay in his hand, emptied of girls to love. I thought about Tinder. I had never even imagined creating a profile. What photos would I use? What smiles? What would I say to people I didn't know? "Hey, how are you? I make music, what about you? Good weather, huh? I keep my T-shirt on because, well, just because I want to." I hadn't ever dared. It would have forced me to talk to girls, though. I felt like I was expected to do it, like the world was searching for the spark of desire deep in my eyes, under my trunks. But in this kind of heat, how could anyone want to get close, to press their skin against someone else's? Even my own skin was unbearable. Sweat trickled down it and I breathed in the stink to intoxicate myself with disgust and the desire to be alone.

The hole was still there. It continued existing, with Oscar inside. I imagined myself posing for a photo in front of it, fingers in a V, with a thoughtful expression, the way some people do because they think it makes them better-looking. A lifeguard climbed up the flagpole to change the color of the flag from green to orange because the waves were getting bigger. The Landes is beautiful, people always said. The air is pure, it's hot, and the ocean is right there. Nobody ever said: The Landes is terrible. It's the fake peacefulness of the pines, the roar of the waves that you know have killed people, and all that laughter, those cries of pleasure, blended into a single muffled echo, like in those badly lit indoor wave pools full of chlorine and dread.

Rising from behind the dune, a red dot appeared in the sky. It rose higher—it was a small kite. For a moment I'd thought it was Luce. The bright red of her sarong against the blue sky. I was thinking about her, I admit it. About her pale skin, which clashed with all the rest. She covered up Louis's words, the noise of the beach. The thought of her made me want to get up.

◆

THE LIFE OF the campsite went on as usual. Pétanque, water aerobics, ping-pong, children falling off bikes and crying. It was a large campsite; hard to remember faces. It was a large village, with its distant streets and neighborhoods. Nobody was keeping count. If anyone went missing, the assumption was that he must be somewhere else. The days when I hid away on my own, nobody had come to look for me. They weren't looking for Oscar, either. Nobody cared if he was dead.

I found Luce by the pool, lying on a plastic sun lounger. She was wearing black sunglasses and drinking Coke. The shade cast a slanting line across her legs. I felt something in my heart. I noticed this because it felt curiously high in my body. Since that morning, everything had been happening lower down, in my stomach: anxiety, cramps, the urge to vomit, etc. Towels were stretched out on two other loungers next to hers; they put me on my guard.

"You came! How was it with your parents?"

"It was fine." I sat at the very end of her lounger, half of my butt hanging over the edge.

"I'm about to leave. I have to go home. You can come with me, if you want."

"Home?"

"To my parents' place. They live nearby. I have to do some laundry. Huh, that's funny, your eyes . . ."

I lowered my gaze.

"Hang on, let me look. It's like they've changed. What color are they? It's hard to tell."

"I don't know."

"Kind of gray . . . with some yellow at the center when you smile. They're nice."

Was she making fun of me? I looked around, on the alert for accomplices, hidden cameras, any explanation for this sudden interest in me. I cleared my throat and blushed in advance.

"You have brown eyes," I said, my voice suddenly going all high-pitched like it did when I first hit puberty.

"Yeah, well observed. They're pretty boring."

I shrugged, like the coward I was. I wished I could say something original to her. The two owners of the towels came back from the snack bar with beers, water streaming down their bare chests.

"Yann and Tom," Luce told me. "This is Leonard. He's a friend."

"Yo."

A friend. They checked me out. I almost left, but I knew I couldn't really.

"It's hot, man!"

"I heard a dog died."

"The one that bit a kid?"

"No, a different one."

I felt the blood fill my head. Yann sat next to Luce. He leaned his arm on her shoulder and she let him. He was handsome, self-assured. I instantly recognized that calmly condescending attitude: in a single glance, he had categorized me as one of those beings who was inferior to him in every respect, yet with a fragility that he supposed meant he had to be kind to me, the way you might water a stunted little plant out of pity.

"I haven't seen you around. Leonard, is it?"

"Yes."

"Like Leonardo DiCaprio."

"Right, yeah." I tried to smile, but it hurt.

"Let's go for a swim . . ."

"Not me," said Luce.

"Okay then, stay here on your own," Yann teased, touching her again. "Coming, Leonard?"

"Not me . . ." I repeated softly.

They laughed.

"Come on!"

"No, I'm fine, thanks."

"You're sweating like a pig!"

"Let him be, man. He doesn't want to swim."

"But look at the state of him—he's melting!"

"I'm fine . . . I'd rather stay here."

"At least take off your T-shirt . . ."

I glanced helplessly at Luce, but she didn't blink. Tom stood up and winked at me, as if to say: Don't worry, fragile little boy, my friend can be a prick, but you'll be fine if you just keep smiling and don't say anything. Yann kept his arm on Luce's shoulder. A memory of last night surged back. I'd watched him in his blue trunks, and I'd wanted to let him die.

"She doesn't want you to touch her," I muttered.

"What?"

Tom started laughing.

"What did he say? What did he say?" Yann repeated. He was laughing, too, trying to pick a fight.

"Nothing," I said coldly. "Go swim."

He slapped me on the face, hard enough to hurt but not hard enough to make me hit him back. Perfectly judged.

"You need to have fun, Leonard."

Tom dragged him toward the pool. Luce stayed where she was, smiling. I was trembling slightly. The tears were pushing up behind my eyes, trying to break them down like doors. Don't cry, I told myself. There's nothing to cry about, is there?

"You were so calm . . . I'd have hit him."

I looked at the campers, all languishing together in the pool, and the fake grass around it, the fake plants, the sun umbrellas, dotted here and there like a 3-D model of the idea of a vacation. The sun, dead overhead, sizzled like a giant lightbulb. I didn't know what I wanted. I could see myself doing things or doing nothing at all, with the same strange surprise in either case. I heard the water aerobics instructor telling people to move their hips to the rhythm of the music to give themselves a perfect body, a perfect body for this summer that was almost over, a perfect body so they could be loved despite their ugly faces, their peeling skin . . . *Jump rope, go, go, jump rope, go, go . . . Easy . . . Take it easy . . . Position one, two . . . Position one, two . . . That's good . . . Yeah, that's good . . .* Something vibrated in my pocket. The same ringtone as last night. Sweat poured down my back like a little waterfall. I took Oscar's phone from my pocket and, hiding it behind my thigh, turned it off. Luce hadn't seen or heard anything. Or maybe she just didn't care. Maybe she didn't care about anything. She sipped her Coke. She suddenly seemed like another person, like one of them. She didn't clash anymore. She, too, was rotting by the pool, this filthy pond. I felt an urge to throw her Coke in her face.

I was sweating too much. I needed to wash myself. Making no attempt to hide what I was doing, I took off my T-shirt for the first time. I had kept it on until then, except in the showers or in my tent, where no one could see me. I was a skinny little runt, my skin marked with tan lines. And maybe with the hands of all the uncles who had slapped me on the back and said: "You need to eat, Leo, you're wasting away!" There was a weird hollow in my sternum. My ribs and shoulder blades stuck out like a little boy's. My thin shoulders led to a long, thin neck that looked as if it would snap like a matchstick. Next to the muscular bodies around me, I was pathetic. A product with no value on the market. But I stood up. I put down Oscar's phone as confidently as if it were mine. I knew that Luce was watching me. I walked over to the pool, head held high, and dived in without pinching my nose. Water flooded my sinuses. I let myself sink toward the bottom. Above me, I saw parts of legs, asses, little feet beating frantically to stay afloat. Filtered through the blue, sunlight and laughter reached me like memories. I could stay there, mouth full of chlorine. One person less at the campsite. No one would notice.

♦

"MY PARENTS THINK camping is beneath them, but they let me come here in summer. I've been camping on my own for the last four years."

"You must know everyone, then."

"No, it changes every year, even if there are a few people who come back. Will you come back, Leonard?"

"I don't know."

♦

LUCE'S PARENTS LIVED in the nearest village. We walked there by cutting through the forest. The path was quiet and shaded. The pine needles were soft and didn't burn my feet. I could still smell the chlorine. I kept my arms away from my body to let the air flow under my armpits. I felt good. I almost forgot about Oscar for a little while. I walked next to Luce and thought about Yann, who had touched her shoulders and who wasn't there anymore. I thought about Oscar, whom she'd gone to find at his bungalow and who wasn't there, either. Oscar, whom she'd kissed the night before. I was jealous. So I thought about Oscar again. But you can't be jealous of Oscar anymore, I told myself, and I stopped thinking about him. I looked at Luce and thought she was pretty. I thought about Oscar, who had probably already walked this path. How could I not think about him? Luce's sarong brushed my hand. The touch went up my arm, all the way to my heart. It was a different kind of heat from the sun. I preferred this one. I wanted to be hot like that.

A couple with their little boy passed us coming the other way. The little boy threatened us with a water pistol. He shot me in the head. Luce laughed. The mother grabbed him and gave him a spanking. He cried. The father looked apologetic and they walked away. Luce started laughing again and I laughed, too. There were beads of water on my face; I was like a wet dog. She reached out a hand to wipe the water away. It ended up as a caress—deliberately, I thought. I let her do it. I wanted to touch her, too, but I didn't know how to go about it. Everything in me started in the gut but withered as it moved toward the outside, falling to pieces by the time it reached my fingertips, which didn't know how to caress. All the same, I lifted my hand. Something in this forest was pushing me. We were far from the campsite and the music. All it took was one sideways step. I caressed her face. I followed its contours, my hand trembling, and that tremble became the caress itself, descending over her eyes, along her nose, her cheeks, her mouth. Luce didn't move. Her eyes were closed. Everything I'd never said, I could finally say, without a sound. I wanted to tell her so much. This wasn't enough. I leaned down to take her in my arms, but she stopped me with a smile and we set off again.

When we reached her street, Luce asked me to guess which house was hers. I saw one with green shutters and pointed at it—I guessed right. Luce smiled. She took my hand and I thought that she was going to lead me to her bedroom. But she stood in front of the open garage door. "Shit, they're home." She let go of my hand.

Her father appeared. "Hello."

"Hello, sir."

"Well, this is it!" Luce said, giving me a friendly pat on the back. "This is where I live!"

"It's very nice."

The father looked at me like I was a stain, then he went inside. Luce had changed. She was embarrassed. She was actually blushing. It made me love her even more. I wanted to get to know her father, to talk to him and make him like me.

"Sorry, it's better if you don't come in. I'll be here for a couple of hours. I can meet you at my tent after if you want."

"Okay."

I hesitated to touch her as I said goodbye. She gave me a quick kiss on the cheek, then she left and I was alone. Oscar returned, with his smell and his dead eyes.

◆

ON MY WAY back through the forest, I still had that anxiety in my guts, but it was different now, more bearable. I smiled. I remembered Luce's face. I remembered her body so close to mine, and her thigh against mine, caressing (without knowing it) Oscar's phone in the pocket of my trunks. Something wasn't right. Something was trying to come out of my mouth. I picked up the phone. I threw myself down in the needles at the foot of a pine tree and dug a small hole. The earth was soft. I put the phone inside and filled the hole. Then I stood up. I vomited—some bile and some pool water—and set off, reeling slightly, toward the campsite. It couldn't be much later than three o'clock. I didn't know what to do until it was time to leave. Brush my teeth, and then? "So, Leo," my father would often say, "what are your plans for today?" I never answered. I had no plans. I followed Louis or my dog along paths, and I waited for the hours to pass, for the suns to set one by one until the last night. Nothing had changed.

I went back to the dune to see the hole. It was already like an old grave. The others around me didn't know. They brushed past death and the end of vacation as they headed toward the beach. Children unknowingly built castles in memory of Oscar. Sometimes a passerby, walking on the burning sand, would grimace with pain, and it was as if they knew. I would look at them then, seeking contact. But they would start smiling again and walk away. At the top of the dune, everyone skirted around a stroller, abandoned in the sun. Some of them leaned down in terror to look inside and saw to their relief that it was empty. Some of them thought it was my stroller. They imagined I was a careless teenager, letting his little brother get burned. They advised me not to stay where I was, in this terrible heat. I told them I was waiting for someone. It was true. In two hours, Luce would return. I clung to that. It was my only marker in this slow, empty day. I waited. And when I couldn't stand the waiting any longer, I wanted to scrape away the sand, revealing the hole to the eyes of the world so that it would finally be over and I would be taken away.

I got bored. I left the dune and wandered around

the campsite for an hour, maybe longer. I moved my lips without speaking. People avoided me. The sound of the speakers was even louder than before. I closed my eyes to drown out the music, which bounced off bodies and tents like light on the dust of the paths. *Des-pa-cito . . . Quiero desnudarte a besos despacito . . .*

"Hey, Leo, what're you doing?"

It was Louis. I was at the pétanque court. All around me, people were kissing, like at the start of an orgy. I thought I was hallucinating, then I remembered: it was "hot blindman's bluff." It happened every Saturday. It was written on the schedule at the reception desk. I even thought: Why didn't I remember that? Why had I walked here, in this state, on a Saturday, in the middle of hot blindman's bluff?

"What're you doing?" Louis repeated. "Do you want to play?"

People were running. The ones wearing blindfolds had to catch them. If they did, they could kiss them. It was saucy and hilarious. People watched, laughing, as the blind ones stumbled in the dust, smiling vacantly, hands reaching out hopefully for all those denied kisses, and all those desperate losers who let themselves get caught on purpose because no one ever saw them otherwise. Somewhere, the pink bunny yelled: "Olé! Olé! OLÉ!" My head started to boil.

"What're you doing?" Louis asked again, louder. Everyone was speaking very loudly.

The bunny appeared out of nowhere to blindfold me.

Des-pa-cito . . . Quiero desnudarte a besos despacito . . . I struggled. He insisted, dancing around, and people stopped to laugh. The animal wanted me to play. Maybe he wanted to strangle me, too. He was hurting me. He didn't blink and he smiled constantly, with that infernal grin drawn on his happy rabbit face. I pushed him away. He fell flat on his face in a cloud of dust. Everyone yelled. Someone shoved me and I fell, too, in front of a waiting pétanque player.

"This is hot blindman's bluff, idiot, not wrestling."

I ran away.

"Get out of here!"

Louis ran after me. "Why the hell did you do that? He didn't do anything to you!"

"He attacked me!"

"He just wanted you to play! You're crazy!"

The music pursued us. As soon as we got away from one speaker, we came close to another.

"Slow down! Why are you walking so fast? You're on vacation, for fuck's sake!"

I kept going until I reached a bench in the sun, far from the pines and the music. My knee was bleeding. I had no car and no bike. I couldn't leave this place. The roads in the Landes were dangerous; nobody walked. I wanted to see the campsite burn.

"What's wrong with you, man?"

"I can't stand this music anymore."

"Oh, I get it . . . Nothing's good enough for Mr. Classical . . ."

He put on a pretentious expression and started humming what was probably the only Vivaldi tune he knew. I thought I was going to hit him. It passed. He stopped humming and leaned against the bench, looking more serious. He made a turban out of his T-shirt. He let a long silence fall and I felt better.

"So, Leo . . . I did it. I fucked Zoe."

"Ah. Well done."

"It was . . . wow."

I got ready to listen. He liked to tell his sad friends how happy he was. It was a pleasure he couldn't resist. Maybe he didn't even realize. He stood straight and his whole body became animated so he could tell me all about it, make me uncomfortable, destroy the little desire that remained to me.

"We went swimming, the two of us . . . We started touching each other . . . I was hard as a rock, man! . . . She said why don't we get out of the sea and go to her place . . . I was ready to do it. I wedged my dick to the side in the elastic of my shorts and put my hands over it to cover the bit that was sticking out. She thought it was funny, too, we were both laughing, and that got me excited . . . After that, I put my T-shirt on and lugged my huge hard-on along all these paths, incognito, in front of kids, old people, maybe even your parents . . . On the way we talked about boring stuff, on purpose, you know, like we didn't know what was going to happen. And then we got to her tent and we kissed and lay down . . . It all happened really fast . . ."

He was out of breath from talking. His whole body

slowed down. He stared into space, and that smile that had lit up his face gradually faded, his lips curling downward as though his joy were melting in the sun.

"It happened too fast . . . Maybe if we'd taken our time a bit more, chatted first or something . . . When I realized it was the moment and I couldn't turn back, I started feeling scared. I thought how important it was, that this was my destiny, I couldn't fail now. I touched myself under my trunks and felt myself getting softer . . . So I thought about porn: Zoe kissed me and I thought about the dirtiest stuff I could remember, gangbangs, double penetration, jizz in the face, and all that. I thought about it to get myself hard again, and it worked a bit, but it wasn't natural . . . It was a struggle . . . I moved my ass away from her so she wouldn't feel that I'd lost my hard-on . . . I was sweating a lot. Bad sweat, you know . . . I wanted to leave . . . I was already thinking that I'd jerk off later and that would be fine . . . So I wanted to concentrate on making her come, at least, but I couldn't even manage that . . . I kept thinking about my dick . . . I rubbed myself against Zoe like a worm . . . I was jerking myself off against her thigh . . . I was kissing her tits, but I wasn't even enjoying it, I wasn't looking at them, I was drooling on them, totally lost . . . After a while my mouth was so dry that it made these horrible sounds when I opened it . . . So I kept it shut . . . I kept giving her these little smiles . . . I was squashing her . . . I couldn't even tell how she was doing on her side . . . We were stuck together, but we weren't really together at all ... We kept trying ... After a while, I tried to stroke her under her bathing suit. But I didn't know how ... I'd seen thousands of pussies before, some of them in close-up, but I had no idea what I was doing, I was lost, I didn't even dare look. I kept getting things mixed up, touching places that didn't do anything ... I wanted to shoot myself ... But then she moaned a bit, and that put me back in the zone. I grabbed the condom and put it on like I'd rehearsed. But it fell off ... I was concentrating so hard, I must have looked ridiculous ... I tried to penetrate her, but I was too rough because I was so scared. My dick bent in two against her belly, it was horrible ... I jerked off a bit and kept smiling at her ... I thought about porn again: in my head I could hear them yelling in English: *Oh yes! Yes! Fuck!* And then in the end she said: 'Don't worry ...' That finished me. I fell onto my back. She pressed herself against me, all sweet. I stared at the canvas looking sort of angry. I kept touching myself with my fingertips, without even realizing ... I wanted to kill people, I swear, I saw myself with a gun, slaughtering everyone in the campsite ... But Zoe just fell asleep ... She was even snoring ... I was hot, I wanted to leave, but I knew that if I moved, she would wake up, and I didn't want that. So I stayed like that, for a long time ... And Leo, you're going to laugh at me, but I swear I was crying."

He closed his eyes and slumped down on the bench. He was breathing more slowly now. I watched the sweat drip from his forehead onto his silver chain, onto his pectoral muscles, onto his Hawaiian shorts and the flip-flops he'd bought at the campsite the first day, grinning like a madman . . . I remembered that, because that was when we met. His chest rose and fell and the gaps between these jolts grew longer, like a wounded animal as it dies. Then he dozed off. Louis always fell asleep when he was too sad. He would wake up afterward and feel fine, ready to get hurt all over again. I felt some empathy. I wanted to pat his shoulder, say something, do something, but nothing came to mind. I tried to imagine what it would be like to be him all the time, but I couldn't manage that, either.

Across from us, a man was folding up his tent. I'd seen him before. He was about forty years old and not very good-looking. One week earlier, he had arrived alone at this camping spot that was too big for one person. He'd filled the space with a table, chairs, and strings of lights. He'd put an antenna in the trunk of his car so he could watch TV in his tent, which most of the campers thought was trashy. He didn't use the TV much, though. He spent a lot of time hanging around outside his tent, watching people go past. Women especially. In the mornings he would go running in the forest. Nobody came to sit on his chairs. His strings of lights kept falling down and he kept putting them back up. Now his vacation was over, and we wouldn't see him again. He would disappear through the archway that he'd appeared through one week before, honking his horn. I watched him, thinking about him and Louis and the others. I let their sadnesses rub against mine. The sunlight blanched all the colors and made the dust shine.

A bent old woman was dragging a cart along the path. "Coke . . . Sprite . . ."

"Yes!" shouted Louis, suddenly opening his eyes. He jumped to his feet, bought a Red Bull, and sat down again. "Oh well, forget Zoe. Who cares! There'll be others . . . So how about you? What's happening with you-know-who?"

I felt afraid. But in slow motion, he silently mouthed into the void: Luce.

"What?"

"Come on. Did you fuck her?"

"No!"

Everything was mixed up. I had a bad feeling. I thought about Luce, it's true. Everything calmed down when I thought about Luce. Inside my head, I repeated her name— Luce, Luce, Luce—so that no other name would appear.

"Did you make out, at least? Fuck, you did! You made out with her! Well done, man. Personally, I don't think she's all that great-looking, but I get that you like her. So what're you doing here? Why aren't you with her?"

"She's at her parents' house," I said in a low voice, ashamed.

"When's she coming back?"

"I don't know."

I knew perfectly well that she would be back in two hours. Or maybe in one hour now, because time had passed.

"So come on, tell me!"

"We were in the forest . . ."

"Shit, I'm already turned on! I'm such a disgusting bastard."

And I felt an iota of pride make its way through me, insinuating its way to the corners of my mouth and stretching it into a smile . . .

"No, nothing happened, really. I don't even know why I'm telling you this."

"Are you serious? You're telling me this because she's your bae."

"She's not my 'bae.'"

"You can be a real pain in the ass sometimes, Leonard. Just loosen up, man!"

"Stop saying that."

I closed my eyes again. I hadn't found a better solution yet. The colors and sounds of the campsite seeped into the darkness. I knew the songs of the birds in the pines and the crunching whine of golf carts on the gravel paths; they had entered my mind and would not leave, like the smell of chlorine from the municipal swimming pool, early mornings in my childhood, and Oscar's eyes, blue on white and circled in blood. I calmly placed my hands over my ears.

Louis took one of my hands and dropped something into it: a condom.

"Here. You'll need it more than me. You've still got time before you leave. But watch out—Luce isn't like you. She's more ... easygoing. She's a shaitan! She changes her mind all the time. Someone could steal her from you at any moment. In fact, they might be stealing her right now! Right ... now!"

He was trying to make me laugh. He grabbed my shoulder and stared at me seriously, and I felt all his compassion, this vast tide of misplaced compassion.

"Don't worry, you can see her again after vacation, anyway. You can add her on Facebook."

"Coke ... Sprite ..."

The woman walked past again. Had she already gone all the way around the campsite? Or was it a different woman?

"Would little Oscar please come to the reception desk right now. His mom is waiting for him so she can go home—and probably give him a good hiding!"

There was a burst of laughter and the microphone went dead. I jumped to my feet.

"Little Oscar," Louis repeated, laughing. "God, how embarrassing."

"I'm going."

"Damn right! Go for it! Give her your sad little smile— that drives 'em crazy. And don't end up like me, eh? Stay hard. Long and hard like Excalibur."

◆

I WANDERED OVER to the reception, where I bumped into Claire, who was coming out of the office. She looked furious—so different from this morning.

"Oh, it's you. Are you here because you heard the announcement?"

I shook my head and took a step back, but she wouldn't let me go.

"Have you seen Oscar?"

"Not since yesterday."

"Were you with him on the beach?"

"Yes."

"Did you go swimming?"

"He did."

She came closer. "Beyond the authorized area?"

"I don't know ... Maybe."

"Do you know what a riptide is?"

"Yes."

"So why didn't you stop him?"

"I don't know ... I'm sorry ..."

My lip started quivering. I suddenly glimpsed the possibility that Oscar had not been strangled but drowned, swept away by treacherous currents. They would search for him in the sea, not in the sand, and they would leave me in peace, unpunished, far from Claire. Her body eclipsed the sun. Every time she moved, beams of light hit me.

"If you know anything, you have to tell me."

"Of course."

"Why did you come to see me earlier? You were acting really weird."

"I was hot . . . I was just passing . . ."

Claire examined my face. I let my head spin from the heat. That way, she wouldn't suspect the truth. She wouldn't see me as just a lost, fragile little boy.

"They're going to call the SNSM."

"Okay," I said without understanding.

"Give me your number. And if you hear anything, call me."

We exchanged numbers. I didn't have anything with me, so she wrote down hers on a piece of paper, which I shoved into my pocket, where Oscar's phone had been before. She gave me one last look and I thought about my lies. She put her hand on my shoulder. Her nails dug into my skin.

"What's your name again?"

"Oscar."

"What?"

"Leonard."

"Are you crazy?"

"Sorry. I just don't feel too good." I pulled myself free from her grip. "I'm hot. And you're making me feel worse.

You're confusing me. I didn't even know your son. Leave me alone."

◆

FOR HOURS, I had been the only one worrying. Nobody had given him a thought, not even his mother. She'd stayed where she was, waiting for him. But the worry was growing now. It would spread through the paths until everyone knew about it. I was scared. I despised myself. I had never been so close to confessing, yet I hadn't done it. I could run away. They might never find me. The sand must have erased my fingerprints. I heard car trunks slamming shut. It was five o'clock, a good time to leave. I could say goodbye to Luce and Louis and just abandon all the rest, like a fire that hasn't been put out properly. I'd wasted enough time.

I went back to our camping spot. My parents still hadn't taken down their tent. That annoyed me. I went into mine to pack my things. Everything was neat and tidy, like a dead man's apartment. How long had I been gone? My clothes were folded in a corner. My electronics were up off the ground so they wouldn't get sand on them. The roll of toilet paper was still hidden behind my pillow. I wondered if I would ever feel like doing that kind of thing again. Sometimes, at night, it was the only way I could get to sleep: wrist moving silently, feet tensed so they wouldn't move the canvas, I would think about all those girls I'd seen who hadn't seen me. And even though I was completely alone, I would blush. Sleep would take me afterward and I'd wake up with no memory of having slept. That was all over now. Farewell, tent, I thought: I'm packing up my stuff and going home and I will never go camping again in my life.

"What are you up to, Leonard?"

"Packing."

"Why?"

"We're leaving soon, aren't we?"

"No."

I went outside and I saw them smiling, as if at good news.

"We've decided not to leave until tomorrow morning."

"My meeting was put back to Tuesday."

"Are you happy?"

"He's not happy . . ."

"Let him speak."

"Leonard?"

I sat down. I nodded and tried to smile. My father was about to say something else, but my mother made a movement with her hand to stop him. She looked at me over her book. I recognized that look, a look that I often only felt, the kind of look she would give me during family meals when someone said something that might hurt me and she would examine me in silence, anxiously monitoring my expression for any reaction. I felt her gaze pierce me softly, passing beyond mirages to grasp the truth in my eyes, and perhaps Oscar's face, which survived somewhere within me.

"Anyway, you need to take Bubble for a walk," said my father. "The poor dog's dying over there."

My mother turned away. She looked around for the dog. "Where is he?"

"Bubble!" shouted Alma. She was standing there, next to me; I hadn't felt her hand on mine. "We have to find him."

"I'll go," I said abruptly.

And I left. Alma ran after me.

◆

"WHAT DO YOU do, Leonard, when you're not with us?"

"I don't know . . . I walk, I see people."

"Who?"

"Friends."

"Who?"

"I have a friend called Louis."

"Oh, the one who sweats? I've seen him."

"Everyone sweats, Alma."

"I don't. Adrien sees people, too, you know."

"I know."

"I think he has a girlfriend."

"That's good."

"Why are you sad today?"

"I'm not sad."

I smiled at her and she looked happy. We continued searching for Bubble. Maybe he'd left the campsite and gone north, toward the beaches with their cool gray pebbles. It was nicer there. I felt a gentle sadness move through me at the thought of never seeing my dog again.

Now I had more hours to get through. The day opened up like a wound. The vacation started over. There would be another night. I could avoid thinking about it, keep walking for a long time with Alma, keep following the paths and searching for Bubble. But the fear would grow. The SNSM, whatever that was, would spread through the campsite. Claire's eyes and my mother's eyes would blend into the same unbearable gaze. Nobody slipped away for two nights running. By the second, you had disappeared. You might even be dead, if they found the body, buried in the sand by my own hands. I thought about erosion. I wasn't sure about the word. Erosion: a breeze comes off the sea, like a whisper in the sand, and reveals Oscar . . . Oscar's open eye staring from the sky.

And then, all of a sudden, I felt fine. These hours and hours were a tunnel. I would walk through it with her—with Luce—until morning.

◆

"CAREFUL ON THE beach, people! The waves are getting bigger and the orange flag might turn red soon. This is the Landes! But waves mean wind, and wind means coolness . . . In fact, I'm hearing in my earpiece that there might be a storm tonight . . . I'll keep you informed!"

Luce was hanging out her freshly washed laundry. "Is that your little sister?"

"Yeah." I felt proud. I wanted Luce to meet her.

"What's your name?"

"Alma. What's yours?"

"Luce."

"Alma," I said, "can you find your way back to Mom and Dad on your own?"

"They said you have to stay with me."

"I know, but I'd rather stay with Luce. You understand?"

"I understand!"

She vanished like a flower. I walked over to Luce, feeling quite emotional. I felt like she'd just returned from a long journey. "I missed you."

"That's nice of you, Leonard . . . What did you do while I was away?"

"Waited for you."

She continued hanging up her laundry. She didn't touch me, barely even looked at me. I paced around near her tent, thinking: What, has she forgotten? I'd thought she would kiss me. Suddenly she burped and came toward me as if I were an old friend.

"Did you hear the bunny? There's going to be a storm. See that, in the sky?"

"What am I supposed to see?"

"Way over there, look. Black clouds. I can't wait. At least it'll break up this crappy routine. Do you want to go swimming?"

"Okay."

She doesn't love me. Not anymore. Those two hours were an eternity for me, but for her they were nothing. She went to wash some clothes and then she came back.

I smiled, trying to stay dignified. I started looking around for cameras again, for a group of people hidden in the bushes ready to jump out and laugh at me. What did she want from me? She was good-looking. Better-looking than me, anyway. If she wanted, she could get a boy who was way calmer and more confident. But she persisted. She gave me her time. This was all I'd wanted, and now I felt guilty. I thought: She's hanging out with me because she doesn't know I killed Oscar. She touched my arm as she went past. I took a step toward her, but she moved away.

"Do you want me to lend you a towel?"

"Okay."

She threw it at my head, then she took my hand and off we went. I followed her awkwardly to the beach. There was no point denying it: I was like a weathervane in her wind; my heart fluttered every time she even glanced at me. Why had I chosen her, this girl who dragged me around like a little dog? I was always too late: sometimes her eyes seemed loving, but before I even had time to believe it, she seemed to ignore me again; then, just as I'd start feeling sad, she would hold my hand. I was at her mercy. If she asked me to jump . . . We passed the hole and I didn't even look at it.

◆

LUCE KISSED ME at about six o'clock, without warning. We looked at each other and she leaned down to take my face in her hands. The beach disappeared; there was nothing but her lips. I lost myself in them. I didn't know what to do, so I tried a few movements that did not match hers. Gradually I got the hang of it. It developed like music; our solos combined. It was a long kiss, and to me it felt like a rebirth, like an immense door opening up in the sky. Afterward, it was just the two of us, but it was like we spread ourselves over the beach so our joy could flow between the bodies on the paths like sunlight. I loved this beach. I played volley-ball. I took off my T-shirt and walked around bare-chested, without waving my arms to cover up my skinniness, without thinking at all, melting into the crowd as if it were water. A plane flew overhead with a banner advertising Fanta, and that made me want a drink. I called out to a soda vendor and bought a can of Fanta to share with Luce. I had be-come part of the system; I was making the most of it, like the others. The smell of donuts and the noise of Jet Skis no longer sickened me. The heat wasn't oppressive; it intoxicated me, made me sweat with pleasure. Luce and I went swimming. The waves cut us down, knocked us over. The lifeguard whistled and yelled at me several times. I laughed. I couldn't feel the sun on my head anymore or the sea that was stronger than I was. I listened to the music and recognized a song: *Vamos a la playa . . . A mí me gusta bailar . . . Sounds of fiesta . . .* When at last my tiredness made everything spin, Luce dragged me back to the towels. I kissed her, then she started reading under the sun umbrella, the shade tracing a delicate line on her legs again. I lay in the sun to tan my body, which now wanted to dance with the others.

"Luce, you coming?" said a boy on his way past.

"No, thanks!"

No, thanks! I couldn't stop smiling. Everything that wasn't me was like water off a duck's back.

"How old are you, Leo? You look young."

"Seventeen."

"One year younger than me, then. And apart from Alma, do you have any other brothers or sisters?"

"I've got a brother. He's fifteen."

"Does he look like you?"

"Not at all."

"Is he good-looking?"

"I don't know . . . I've never thought about it . . ."

I frowned, which must have made me look stupid, because she laughed. What did she want from me? She came closer.

"I don't know anything about you. Like ... what was the best day of your life?"

"Probably the day my parents gave me Bubble. My dog."

"Would you sell Bubble for a lot of money?"

"Never."

"Is there anything that really disgusts you?"

"Um ... inequality, maybe."

"Yeah, you're right. Inequality is really bad. You'll be old enough to vote at the next election ... Will you?"

"No."

"Why not? Because you don't understand enough about it?"

"No, because I don't feel like it."

"What do you feel like doing?"

"I don't know ..."

"What do you want, deep down?"

"I don't know ... I don't know."

I was embarrassed. That amused her.

"It's okay if you don't know. Anyway, maybe you're only interested in your music at the moment."

"Thanks."

"So what kind of music do you listen to?"

"A bit of everything ..."

"I always want to slap people who say that."

"Sorry. I like ... classical music."

"I don't know much classical music, but I love Chopin."

"Chopin isn't really classical music, technically speaking," I corrected her, blushing. "It's more like romantic music."

She smiled and tilted her head apologetically. I wanted her to keep asking me questions.

"Okay, so I like romantic music, then. What else would you recommend? Something that goes well with the moment."

I thought about it while looking out at the beach. Melodies collided in my mind and I felt good. I felt I belonged here as much as anyone else.

"Maybe the prelude to *Lohengrin,* by Wagner."

"I'm going to listen to that right now."

She took out her earbuds and her phone and looked it up on YouTube. I went into a panic at the idea that she wouldn't choose a good version, that her earbuds wouldn't do justice to the sound, especially here, that she would be disappointed. I wanted to tell her not to listen to it, but I forced myself to stay quiet. I didn't want to ruin the moment. After finding the music, she lay on her back, hands over her ears, eyes closed. I was alone. Luce was listening to the prelude to *Lohengrin* on my beach of suffering, which was now my beach of bliss. I couldn't believe it. The piece lasted about nine minutes, sometimes longer—it depended on the conductor. Would she listen to the whole thing? I hoped she would wait until the forty-sixth bar. I knew she wouldn't open her eyes right away, so I watched her without fear for a long time, and as she listened, I followed the music on her face and on the beach. It felt as though all of us were held in suspense, Luce and me and the others, as if we were one gigantic body lying on the sand, waiting for something to happen. Had Luce reacted to the forty-sixth bar? I heard the strings quiver and I couldn't hold it back any longer. Hot tears filled my eyes, blurring everything. The joy came to a head, and everything slid downward into peace, into silence. Luce sat up. I heard the sound of waves and shouting again.

"Not bad at all. Thanks."

"Thank you for taking the time to listen to it."

"Why did you choose that piece of music?"

"I don't know . . . It just seemed obvious."

"When you talk about music, your eyes change. It's like everything's better."

I didn't know what else to say. A pleasant tightness squeezed my heart, prevented me from speaking. I looked at her. I thought she was fantastic—that was the word that came to mind: fantastic. But I knew nothing about her. I had answered her questions and she had listened to me. I wanted to ask her things, too, but she beat me to it.

"You're not happy at this campsite, are you, Leonard?"

"I'm happy right now."

"Let's take a photo, then!"

Without waiting, she lifted up her phone and took a selfie, arms outstretched to get us both in the frame. She showed it to me, and I realized that I would never forget our faces, no matter what happened afterward: Luce looking away, her face pensive, and me smiling shyly. She lay down and closed her eyes.

"Luce? Actually, my parents have decided to stay one more day. I'm not leaving until tomorrow morning."

"That's cool. Let's sleep a bit now. And you should lie in the shade."

I tried to sleep, because she wanted me to.

I wished there were more music. A long time had passed since dawn: the sun had crossed the sky and was already drifting toward the sea; soon it would disappear behind it, taking with it all those frustrated desires, those caresses never given, those words never spoken. Around us, people continued to laugh and run. The tide was rising. We had to hurry to be happy. I remembered a book that my parents used to read to me when I was a child, *La Chèvre de Monsieur Seguin*, about a brave little goat who fought hard to drive back a wolf during the night. I had heard the story many times—I knew exactly how it ended—but I would always hope: "From time to time, the stars danced in the clear sky and the goat thought: 'Oh, if only I can hold out until dawn ...'" I remembered each word, and the sadness returned with them. With my eyes closed, I could no longer feel the sunlight; I could imagine that it was another time of day, that we were somewhere else, and that nothing was dead.

◆

I WAS WOKEN by a feeling of hardness inside my trunks. Something was straining against the fabric. I lay facedown. No one had seen me. Luce was still asleep. I was covered in sweat and my head ached. I must have gotten sunstroke. Down below, the hardness kept pressing against my towel. This had never happened to me at the beach. I didn't understand. It was actually painful. My eyes were fixed on Luce. I wasn't looking at her face but at her breasts and the curve of her butt under her swimsuit. I felt stronger, more stable. I moved toward her and kissed her, stroked her with my fingertips, shivering with a new kind of heat that had nothing to do with the sun or with anxiety but was something else altogether, irresistible.

"Leo."

"Luce . . ." I kept caressing her, my fingers trailing over her stomach.

"Leo. We're at the beach."

"Then let's go back . . ."

"No."

I wanted to stop but I couldn't help myself.

Luce suddenly sat up. "What are you doing?"

I pulled a face, embarrassed. She looked away.

Yann and Tom, the two boys from the pool, spotted us from a distance and came over to join us. I put on Luce's sunglasses to hide my eyes in case I started crying. They checked me out. Yann sat between us and Tom on the other side, close to me.

"Jesus, this motherfucking heat . . . How you doing?"

I nodded behind my sunglasses. They were very practical. I wanted to listen to what Luce was saying, but one towel's length was enough distance not to hear anything but the waves—and Tom talking to me with his breath that smelled of beer and fries.

"So ... are you with her or not?" He gestured to Luce.

I shrugged. I felt eloquent, without saying a word.

"Did you make out?"

"Yeah."

"Did you fuck her?"

"No."

"It's hard work with her. Yann's struggling, look at him ... Oscar had a hard time, too, you know. She sent him packing last night. He was pissed off, man ... I bet that idiot puked. I think he left with his mother without even saying goodbye. Look at the sky ... There's a storm coming. It's going to explode. Hey, are you listening to me?"

A lifeguard was yelling. All swimmers had to get out of the water: it was getting dangerous. I sensed Yann moving closer to Luce, trying to seduce her with his words. What's the point? I thought. Go ahead and try. Anyway, everything was going to explode. The storm would coincide with a massive wave that would sweep away the beach, the campsite, and all the tangled desires of the girls and the boys. A red helicopter was hovering near the water. That was the SNSM. They were checking to see if Oscar's corpse was floating in the sea. They were looking in the wrong place.

They were searching the sea because the sea was obviously violent and cold. The sand, by contrast, was too soft and warm; Oscar couldn't be there. They'd gotten the wrong enemy, just like I'd mistaken the smiles and the laughter, the joy spreading along the paths. Everywhere, it was the same big misunderstanding. Not many people committed suicide in the water. The helicopter flew farther out to sea and I stayed where I was, in the sun, still hard against my towel.

◆

THE TWO OF us walked back to her tent without speaking. I sat next to her and lowered my head.

"You're an idiot, staying in the sun like that."

"Sorry."

"You're kind of weird, you know. I mean, I like you, but you do some weird things."

"Sorry . . ."

"Say it again."

"Sorry."

"I'm kidding. I get it."

She let me kiss her. Even a pretty chaste kiss sent shivers through my skin and made me start moving my hips despite myself. I was ridiculous: driven into ecstasy by the slightest touch. My breathing grew faster. She kissed me more deeply. Her hand slid up my thigh. I pressed myself against it. We were sweating. I caressed her breasts. Her other hand grabbed my throat.

"Leo . . ."

I looked at her and I didn't recognize her.

"Leo, what the fuck do you think you're doing?"

She pulled away, but I grabbed her hand. I could feel my skin more than hers—that's what happens when you touch someone who doesn't want to be touched. Luce punched me in the ribs. I bent over, doubled up in pain. I didn't know what to do. Finally I stood up. She wasn't the same: her mouth was tense, her forehead creased. She didn't look pretty anymore.

"You should see your eyes . . ."

"You're playing with me," I said very quietly. "You make me think there's something between us, but there's nothing."

"Poor Leonard."

"Like you did with Oscar," I muttered.

She gave this terrible little laugh, worse than the punch. I almost told her that Oscar was dead: Anyway, Oscar's dead.

"Go away."

I did. Luce vanished and the whole campsite took her place: the dust, the barbecue smoke, the yells, the pétanque balls heavy enough to smash a skull, and still—always—the music. *I gotta feeling . . . That tonight's gonna be a good night . . . That tonight's gonna be a good, good night . . .*

◆

NOW THERE WAS only Oscar. He stuck to me, like stagnant water. He clung to my skin. At times I no longer knew how long he'd been dead, how long I'd been dragging him around with me along the paths. Besides, wasn't I guilty long before the moment of his death? Hadn't I had a premonition, from childhood, that everything was leading me toward all this? Nothing was new. All lines converged on this campsite where Oscar had been buried forever. All the distractions and tricks to forget it had now stopped working. The trips the campers made were short: to go get water, to go lie down on a deck chair, to go grab a beer from the icebox . . . I needed something longer. I paced around. "I killed Oscar," I whispered sometimes, so quietly that the confession was only for me. And I thought: *Me,* yes, I'm here, I'm staying, I'm not giving up on myself.

I wanted to take a shower. I hadn't washed since the morning before. I was dirty. Too many different sweats were mixed up on my skin. Near the toilets, I saw my brother, Adrien, kissing a girl under a fake plant. He pulled away from her, looking embarrassed. "Hi, Leo. What are you doing here?"

"Walking," I said, pointing at the path. I looked at the girl who was waiting behind him. She looked embarrassed, too. She was about his age—fifteen. Pretty.

Adrien lowered his voice. "Please don't tell Mom and Dad."

I looked at him, my brother, with his checkered espadrilles, his perfect tan, and his little blue bracelet that he hadn't cut off, that didn't fill him with shame. He was fine here. He blended into the landscape. He was on vacation, so distant from me. My brother the stranger, too happy to wonder anything. And now he was begging me with his puppy dog eyes, as if he knew nothing about all the poor and dying people in the world.

"Why would it matter if I told them?"

He was scared. "I don't know ... I'd just rather you didn't say anything."

"You don't think you're allowed?"

"Stop!"

"Don't worry, I won't say anything."

I stepped to the side to get a better look at the girl. So this was the one he'd kissed, the one he'd make love with if he hadn't already ... Young people, I thought, are doing it earlier and earlier these days. How had they met? Who had made the first move? I felt a stab of envy. It was because of this, I knew, that nothing went right for me. It was because I didn't have a girl who loved me that I had gone astray that night, walking the paths ...

"Why are you staring at her like that? Leo, you're being weird."

"You can go," I replied, like a policeman saying, Move along now.

Adrien nodded coldly and they went. His girlfriend gave me a look that was shy at first, then suspicious, contemptuous, even, as if all it took was a change of angle and she no longer saw me as an authority figure but merely a failed older brother, backward, taller than Adrien but smaller in every other way. I hadn't moved from under the plant. I felt pleased with myself, certain that getting them away from here would prevent them loving each other elsewhere.

The showers were in a raised square covered with a Chinese-style roof. You went in directly from outside. While I was standing in line, a girl came up to me. It took me a moment to recognize her: it was Zoe. Louis's Zoe. She took a big drag on her cigarette. One day she would suck the smoke so hard that it would kill her. I could tell that she was interested in me. It was a rare enough event that I felt pretty sure. I stared at a point close to her, which enabled me to watch as she shot furtive looks at me, never quite sure if I was looking at her, too. She couldn't stand it anymore. I wasn't the only one. People couldn't leave here without having done anything—a cock in the pocket, as Louis put it. You had to fuck at least once, even if it was sad, just once to make the most of the vacation, so you could leave in peace, lightened, unburdened. Under the doors of the cubicles, I spotted the tensed feet of the ones who were masturbating. All the frustrated desires ended up here, discharged against the walls with a stifled yell, washed down into the drains below.

"Hey, you're Louis's friend, aren't you?"

"Yep."

"How's it going?"

"Fine."

"You're lucky . . ."

She waited for me to ask how she was. I let her simmer for a while, taking a cruel pleasure in her discomfort that wasn't like me at all. In the end, she cracked: "I'm not doing so well. I'm not with Louis anymore."

"Oh? I'm sorry."

"Don't worry about it. So . . . are you still with Luce?"

"No."

She shook her head sadly. A cubicle was vacated.

"Shall we go in together?" she said quickly, without looking at me. "It'll save time."

I followed her inside. Some of the people in the line wolf-whistled. I stood under the cold water and closed my eyes. It was nice. I felt Zoe move closer. Her hands stroked my arms. Her thigh slid between mine. Her breasts pressed against my chest. She kissed me, immediately leveraging my mouth open and shoving her tongue inside. I felt like I was kissing an ashtray, but I kept going. I grew excited. An entire body was opening itself up to me. I could do it here, quickly, fill the void that weighed down my life so I wouldn't have to talk about it anymore. My hands moved over her body, and our jerky movements soon got me hard. But then I thought about Luce and about Oscar, Luce and Oscar together, and there were so many moving parts that I suddenly had the impression that there were four of us in that cubicle, all trying to have sex. I opened my eyes. Zoe didn't stop. She was rubbing me aggressively, pressing my hands against her body. She kept going, doggedly determined. The water streamed down her face. She looked like she was crying. Abruptly I pulled away. "I can't."

She couldn't believe it. She tried to smile. "You want me to . . ."

I left the cubicle in a hurry and the door hit me in the nose. I heard Zoe insulting me. Outside, the people in line stared at me and laughed like hyenas. I thought they were all vile, with their colored towels around their flabby, skinny, muscular bodies, all tanned up to their ears, happy to get cleaned up before drinking cocktails, happy to be happy, and yet all of them sad and lonely in the crowd, all of them as lonely as this crappy three-star campsite—it would lose all three stars instantly when Oscar's corpse was found. At least I would have done something good.

I fled. My nose was bleeding. Never tilt your head back! my father always said when I had a nosebleed, so I kept it bent forward, blood dripping on the paths. Like bread crumbs, so I could find my way back. What was making my nose bleed? Stress, the heat, a fragile constitution, a door in the face, or all of the above? Someone handed me a tissue. I stuffed it into my nostril, leaving a crack so that the blood could keep trickling out. I was emptying myself. I was still dirty and I didn't care. Before, it had been a real pleasure—one of the few—to come out of the showers feeling clean and to dry myself perfectly from head to foot so there wasn't a single grain of sand to rub against my flip-flops. Now I didn't care. I had lost everything, down to my tiniest little obsessions.

In the main square, they were getting ready for the evening concert. Bare-chested volunteers were building the stage. They'd brought trampolines for the bungee jump, bounce houses, slot machines, and arcade games. They'd kicked up a cloud of dust. People were getting annoyed. Ten hours of torpor in the sun were waiting to explode like the coming storm. The heat ran through our veins now. The sky was excessively blue, electric. Someone was tuning a guitar. The bunny was herding the campers, like doomed cattle, toward the noise of the machines, the speakers blaring music, the Coke, the fries, the sticky cotton candy, and all that stuff that made me vomit—and yet I was there, too: I was crossing the square. The others must have thought I was already drunk, with the tissue in my nose, my eyes wide open . . . *She's nothing like a girl you've ever seen before* . . . A police van was parked near the reception building. So there we were. It was an investigation now. The helicopter above the sea was no longer enough. They had to check whether Oscar was dead on land, strangled, dragged, folded, buried in the sand. They would find me. It was a news story. The papers were on the presses, waiting. My face would be plastered over the lurid hoardings of the campsite kiosk and beyond. My devastated parents would be asked if they could carry on living after this. If you typed my name into Google, the same photo would appear a hundred times over, my eyes filled with an imaginary horror; they would dig up my old kindergarten class photo and ring my face in red and say: "It was him, that one there . . ." They would forget all the rest. They'd forget these interminable hours and my love. Perhaps I would get a short Wikipedia entry, vaguely mentioning my birth before skipping straight to the crime, passing over sixteen years and arrowing in on Oscar's death, the trial, prison.

I looked for a policeman near the van. I wanted to talk to him, to confess all, be done with this whole mess. But there was no one there. So I found myself looking at Yann, standing by the slots. He was serene—not a problem in the world—with his plastic cup of beer and his gang of friends and his smile, which never vanished. I headed toward them.

"Hey, I need Luce's number."

"Well, look who it is!"

They all snickered at the state of my face.

"What for?" asked Yann.

"I want to text her."

"Why don't you just talk to her in person?"

"I don't know where she is."

"Just go and find her."

"Please just give me her number."

I relaxed, I let myself go. I heard myself speak, saw

myself sway from side to side, tasted the blood in my mouth.

"What do you want to say to her?" Yann demanded. He looked at the others while chewing some imaginary gum. How could they be so predictable, I thought, so ridiculous? Most kids our age united around guys like Yann. Something in their eyes or the timbre of their voice gave them the natural aura of a leader. They radiated something warm and incandescent from their surface, and that was enough to light up other people's eyes, even if, inside, guys like Yann were always cold and empty, with no music in their souls.

"Answer my question, man."

"I asked for her number."

"Luce doesn't give a shit about you. What are you expecting? You think you might finally lose your virginity?"

"Ooooooh!" moaned the others.

"No, I love her," I said with a little smile.

That disturbed them. I enjoyed the moment. I wanted things to degenerate.

"You're completely fucking nuts! Go home."

"What, you don't believe she loves me? Who does she love, then? Yann? No . . . Oscar, maybe?"

Yann took a step forward and shoved himself against me. A jubilant murmur spread through the others and they gathered around us. Louis appeared from nowhere. He stumbled, then grabbed Yann by the arm. "Leave him alone!"

"Fuck off, homo."

Louis was trembling, but he didn't back down. He looked at me without recognizing me because I was smiling at him like I smiled at the others. Yann shoved him onto the ground. "FIGHT!" yelled someone behind me. I charged at Yann. A few people tried to stop me, but others defended me. All the punches I'd never thrown, all the punches I'd received, all the punches I'd dreamed about, and all those I'd seen given unfairly, all of this came down on Yann. I'd never been in a fight before because I was afraid of getting hurt, of damaging my fists. But without that fear, victory went to the maddest, to the one who really wanted to hurt, to mutilate. I hit Yann, and in his eyes I saw Oscar's; I hit him harder and the memories returned: I saw myself watching Oscar and I hit out again. Arms grabbed me and pushed me away. The bunny and other staff members got involved. They broke up the fight. Yann lay on the ground, covered in blood. My face wasn't bleeding. The blood was on my hands.

"You belong in a fucking asylum, you nutcase!"

The bunny took Yann to the infirmary. I walked away. No one dared approach me, not even Louis. I went down a path, one of those paths I'd walked along dozens of times that day. I couldn't take it anymore. People stood like hedges and watched me pass. Some of them insulted me; they wanted to tear me apart, eat me. Maybe they knew. Maybe they guessed that Yann was nothing, that the few punches I'd thrown at his face were nothing compared to Oscar, who had died because of me. All around me, the net was closing. Yet no one came to arrest me. The police were busy searching elsewhere. I was still free and even the night was slow in coming, like a knife pressed gently against my throat.

◆

INSIDE MY SMALL tent, all was calm. Early evening. It was bearable. The shadows and the sounds slid over the canvas. People passed by, unsuspecting. I tried to breathe slowly. Visions of caresses and sand mingled in my mind. I couldn't keep them away anymore. Outside, the waves kept crashing; I could hear them in the distance. It didn't stop. The pink bunny would prance around tomorrow and the days that followed. After August, August would come around again. As during all those insomniac nights, the air thick with moisture and mosquitoes, my hand slipped inside my trunks. A dose of endorphins to help me fall asleep. Jerking off several times, without desire or pleasure, until exhaustion. But I couldn't even do it anymore. Everything was limp. I heard singing through the canvas. They were having fun. A long line of people dancing around my tent. So what is the difference, I wondered, between this and all those other times when I've hidden here, waiting for people to go away? What has changed since then? I'm a little older. I kissed a girl, then lost her. Oscar died. Oscar is dead because he wanted to die, because he was sad and he had the idea of coiling the ropes around his neck to make something happen. Oscar is dead because of all those people who didn't understand him. Oscar is dead because of me, because I did nothing. Because I didn't move. And I didn't move because, at that moment, I couldn't. I would rather have died like him, and we could have watched each other die while the others danced.

◆

"LEO . . . LEO . . ."

A hand touched my tent and opened the flap. Louis's face appeared, his lip split by Yann's fist. He had Bubble on a leash.

"I found your dog . . . He was hiding under a bush . . . I'm going to tie him to a tree, okay?"

Okay. He was calm. He wasn't hassling me. The sun was lower in the sky; that was good. Louis tied Bubble to a pine and returned to the tent. "Can I come in?"

He sat in my tent, cross-legged. The space was too cramped for two people unless they were lying next to each other.

"He was near one of the bounce houses. There's some cool air that comes out the back of it. Dogs love that."

I smiled to say thank you. It pulled on my skin.

"Are you okay, Leo?"

"I'm great."

"Thank you for protecting me . . . when I tried to protect you . . . earlier."

He looked at my body. He didn't dare tell me that I was red and dirty.

"After the fight, I saw Luce in the square. I talked with her. She told me what happened between you two, what you did . . . Anyway, I'm not judging you. But I could tell that she liked you and she thought it was a shame. I think you should go and see her, to say sorry. Maybe it'll make things better."

"I don't care."

"Well, she does."

"Stop talking about it."

"I know you love her really."

I moved my head. It came suddenly, without warning.

"Don't cry, man."

I cried. It went on for a long time. It made furrows in the dust. Louis took me in his arms. I kept crying against him. His hands were on my shoulders. They went down my arms and held my hands. He touched his fingertips to mine. His head leaned against my neck. He kissed me there, trembling. I didn't understand. I had never understood—never noticed—the way Louis had been looking at me, all that time. The sun had made me stupid. It had numbed my brain, leaving only my skin to feel. What had he been doing all day? He kissed me again so he wouldn't have to look at me. I didn't stop him. I just felt two wet lips—and all the sadness and loneliness that stirred in this campsite below the sound of laughter and waves. I gently withdrew my hands. He didn't move. He was in suspense, his face against my neck. Finally he sat up. His eyes were red, too. He smiled to stop himself from crying. "Sorry."

"I need to sleep."

"I'll go."

He left. His shadow passed to the other side of the canvas. I felt a sudden urge to tell him everything. He came back. "Leo, don't say anything. Please."

I promise, I thought. Or maybe I said it, very quietly. I promise: I won't say anything about you . . . or about Oscar. I won't say anything at all except the usual clichés when people ask me how I am. I swallowed my confession like a ball of mucus. He waved his hand as if in farewell. He wasn't going far, though. You couldn't leave the campsite just like that. There was one night left. This vacation would crush us in its grip until the very end.

I lay down and fell asleep.

◆

MY PARENTS WOKE me. They'd just come back from an excellent bingo evening, with drinks. They'd won a coupon to come back to the campsite in October. They thought I seemed listless. The temperature was so pleasant at this time of day. Why wasn't I outside with the others? To cheer me up, they suggested we go eat dinner at the best restaurant in Dax. We wouldn't be back too late; I'd still have time to enjoy the last evening with my friends, maybe even my girlfriend . . .

"Stop."

◆

IT'S EASY TO spot other campers when they go out in town. They look around as if they're rediscovering everything. They leave sand behind as they walk. They don't pay attention to traffic lights when they cross the street, and sometimes they almost die, because they're arriving from another world; they've forgotten the rest.

The sun was setting. I, too, had forgotten. All that day, there had not been just the campsite, trapped between the road and the sea. I saw buildings again, buses, electric lights, I heard snatches of conversation as people walked past. Step by step, I expanded my loneliness. It wasn't just at the campsite that no one knew. Everywhere, no one knew. I had forgotten about the streets and the other countries, this world that continued spinning while I was burying. Beneath the sand, Oscar was the center of that world. I could distance myself from it. When the horizon opened up, I saw other cities in the distance and highways. Escape routes. We had come here by car; we could leave by car, too. My family and Bubble were walking quietly alongside me. I could have suddenly thrown a fit: curled up in a ball and screamed like a child until they agreed to cancel this final night and go home immediately. It was feasible, if I forced it. But I was hungry. I'd hardly eaten anything since the day before. I wanted a steak and fries, with the obligatory salad that you never touch. One small pleasure, at least. Afterward, I thought, we'll see.

♦

MY PARENTS WERE finishing their desserts. I was slumped in my seat, half-asleep. I'd eaten a lot and drunk a lot of wine to make myself feel better. My parents liked it when I drank wine. I looked at my phone: nothing. No one knew I'd gone to Dax, no one was wondering where I was. Luce had forgotten me.

"You're not very chatty, Leonard."

"Can I go see the fish in the aquarium?" Alma asked.

"Yes, but don't go anywhere else."

She left.

"You could make an effort, Leonard. It's our last night, too, you know."

"I'm going outside to call someone," said Adrien.

He left and I found myself alone with them. Their four eyes were fixed on me. My mother smiled and took a breath. "We understand that your thoughts are elsewhere at the moment . . . We just hope that everything's okay. With your friends, I mean, and . . ."

"And your girlfriend?" my father added.

My mother gave him a sharp look. I thought about all those times when they'd asked me about my "love life." Stop asking me about that. I don't have a love life. If I did, I'd tell you.

"Anyway," said my father, who was also a bit drunk, a state that always made him want to talk very honestly, "if we're cramping your style, you should tell us . . . I mean, for example, if you wanted to, um . . ."

"Bring someone back to my tent?" I said abruptly.

My mother laughed nervously. My father shrugged and smiled. "Well, yeah, for example."

"To do what?"

They were embarrassed. I was finally giving them what they wanted and they were embarrassed. They started sweating like they were out in the sun.

"To sleep with a girl?"

My mother hurriedly looked away, but my father laughed lasciviously and gave me a frank, unshockable look. "Well, yeah, for example . . . I mean, that's up to you, Leo . . ."

"No, I'm not interested in that."

My mother took another breath. I sensed that something was coming.

"Listen . . . whatever your . . . your 'orientation' . . . we would never judge you, Leo. Never."

"God, you're stupid! It has nothing to do with that."

"Leo, what's gotten into you?"

"I just don't want to, okay? Girl, boy, I don't care."

They didn't understand. I was enjoying this conversation. I wanted them to feel bad, too. I also wanted them to stop talking to me about sex while blushing. I finished the wine in their glasses. My father grabbed my arm.

"Leo, what's going on?"

"Let me go." I pushed him away.

"We're just trying to help you!"

"No, you just want me to bring a girl home. That's all you think about!"

There was a silence. Some of the other customers were watching us. My father stood up slowly and went to pay the check. Alma was clueless. She stared at me from the other end of the restaurant, frowning, one hand touching the glass wall of the aquarium. My mother concentrated on not bursting into tears. Then gave me an insistent look, as if demanding that I tell her everything, now, tell her everything that was on my mind, once and for all, while we were alone. She took hold of my hands and squeezed them. I was on the verge of tears. It was too much in one day. I almost spoke then, but . . . no, damn it, my mouth stayed shut. It was impossible. That's all there was to it.

Outside, it was dark. Adrien was standing under a streetlight, talking on the phone. It was already late. My phone buzzed and my heart jumped. It was a text, my first of the day: *Louis gave me your number. Come to the beach—there's a party. Luce.*

◆

WE DROVE BACK to the campsite, gliding along those endless Landes roads, bordered by dark pine trees. No one dared say anything. Bubble was panting close to me. Alma was holding my hand. I could feel Adrien's cold gaze on me. I stared at the dashboard lights and listened to the warm voice of the radio. A journalist was talking about the heatwave: a climatic event on an extraordinary scale, the worst to hit Europe since 2003. In France, many people had died. The government was on vacation. The lessons of the past had not been learned. The bonds of society were breaking. A political crisis was looming. My father turned off the radio. What did we know about the damage caused by the heat? For two weeks, we had lived without television or Internet, using our phones only to check what time it was when we were on the beach. Except Adrien. Maybe he knew how many people had died, but he didn't say anything. We were cut off from the world. Beyond the campsite, France was in the grip of a crisis. Oscar was not alone. The heat had ravaged the country. When the silence grew too oppressive, my mother turned the radio on again. Some journalists were still arguing about society, and then it was the weather: "The expected storms will spare the Southwest and move northward. On the coast, however, the wind from the west will reach fifty miles per hour during the night, creating a heavy swell with significant tidal coefficients. Prudence is advised in the sea and on the beach."

In the main square, the concert was in full swing. The campsite's rock group was playing "Jump" by Van Halen. It didn't sound very good. They didn't have a synthesizer to do those big chords in the introduction, so they played them on the trumpet. I could hear it from the car while we drove past the square. There were parents there, some children, and a few stray teenagers: the losers of the campsite, the ones who preferred Coke to beer, a gentle village fete to a rowdy beach party; the weak, the lame, the oppressed, the resigned, the ugly, the repressed homosexuals, the fat boys, the fat girls, the foreigners, the ones who were still too young, the ones who were already too old ... they were all mixed up with the parents and children to spare themselves pain. Here, they were all happy and yet, at the same time, all lost, fucked over, left on the sidelines of adolescence.

Our car moved away. My phone buzzed several times.

Luce called me and I didn't answer. I wanted her to think I was dead.

We parked near our tents. The string lights looked pathetic. My parents wanted to talk to me again, to find out what was going on with their son, but I left.

I ran toward the dune. Little by little, the electronic dance music on the beach drowned out the rock music from the campsite. I ran faster, in time with the bass beats. The paths were empty, the colors had disappeared. The tents and the bungalows were lost in shadows. It was the same night as the one before. Oscar had been dead for almost twenty-four hours. The same night, except for the wind and the impression that I had been on a long journey. Suddenly I thought that the body was not well hidden. As crudely concealed as a child behind a curtain. All it would take was some wind and the sand would blow away, revealing fabric, skin, bruised neck. I thought about that now. I thought about it now because maybe I had wanted it to be badly hidden before, so that someone would find it without me having to help them. But now I had to bury it better. So deeply that it would not be discovered until an archaeological dig in the future, when nothing would remain of the body but bones, an old memory, and I would be dead, this campsite gone. A large plastic shovel was leaning against a bungalow. I grabbed it as I passed, like a javelin. Something in the music drew me toward the dune with fear and jubilation, the two feelings mixed up in my face, or alternating, maybe, in rhythm with the streetlights that illuminated each intersection. I climbed the dune. The sand was warm. My city shoes sank into it. High above, the horizon opened up to reveal bright little dots: a fire, phone screens, the foam of the waves in moonlight. There was no storm, just a warm wind and a huge swell forming out at sea. The tide was high. The party was taking place on what remained of the beach. Scattered figures drinking and dancing. The bunny, a pink glow in the darkness, was carrying the speaker that sent the bass beats in muffled waves up to my ears. The dance music made something rise in my chest. It petrified me with anxiety. It was the music of the dead, the music of tragedy. It reminded me, too, of those porn stars who pound away endlessly at orifices, eyes bulging, veins throbbing, fit to burst. For an instant I wanted to yell at them all down below, to tell them that the music they were listening to was horrible, and that Oscar was dead. I didn't dare go down the dune. I wanted to run away. But think about Oscar, I kept telling myself. Stay focused on Oscar. Don't listen to the music. Bury Oscar so deep that you will forget him. Move his body without fuss, as if you were just doing some DIY at home on a Sunday. And maybe it is Sunday already. It's past midnight. There's not much time left.

I walked down the dune, searching for the lifeguard's flag. I couldn't find it. They must have taken it out so the wind didn't blow it away. Now I didn't know where anything was. Everywhere I looked, it was just sand. I turned on the light on my phone and examined the ground. I got down on all fours and searched everywhere. I could hear shouting from the beach. Something was happening. I kept scraping away, like a dog, like the night before, exactly the same but in reverse, because Oscar was on the other side of the ground. Someone moaned. There he is, I thought. A few feet below, a figure was crawling. I approached it, trembling, shovel in hand in case it attacked. But it wasn't Oscar. It was some stoned teenager dragging himself along on his belly as if his legs had been cut off. He laughed when he saw me. "Tsunami . . . Better watch out . . ."

A very small wave wet our feet. The boy was laughing so much, he swallowed a mouthful of salt water and almost choked. The swell out at sea was so enormous that the waves were now reaching the dune. I dropped the shovel and headed toward the lights. Where was Oscar? There was a second wave and the water came up to my calves. I found myself in the middle of the crowd, surrounded by laughter and yells, the wind, the bass beats, and the sound of the water rising, flooding everything. People were still dancing. Someone was holding the speaker above his head. Everyone was excited. Some fell, then reappeared farther out, laughing hysterically. It was dangerous. The riptides. Someone could die. Where was Luce? I wasn't searching for Oscar anymore. The sea would reach him. It would suck him up and deposit him somewhere else. I swayed between the dancers. I was dancing, too, to avoid the waves. At last I was dancing, without shame or fear. Someone handed me a drink. I swallowed it. The alcohol warmed me inside. I drank some more. The bunny recognized me. "Hey, it's you! You were the one who shoved me this afternoon! You beat that kid up in the square! What the hell is wrong with you, you little prick?"

He raised his paw to hit me, but in the end he held me gently in his arms and murmured into my ear: "All is forgiven . . . Here, all is love . . ."

I remained pressed against his fur, soaked with alcohol and filth. Suddenly he started laughing and let me fall. He vanished into a whirl of lights and yelling. I almost yelled, too. Maybe I did. Car headlights were shining down on the party.

"The sea will soon cover the entire beach. Come back to the campsite." A voice through a megaphone addressing us from the top of the dune. "Do not try to find your belongings. Come directly to the campsite."

People started climbing the dune. They shoved past me as I sat on the ground. Bottles and items of clothing were floating everywhere. Maybe Oscar was floating, too. The music and the lights moved into the distance. I was left alone. The water covered me. The backwash sucked me away from the dune and I drifted, slowly, through the cold water and out to sea. I wasn't breathing anymore. In brief moments I could catch glimpses of sky. The water was entering my mouth and my nose. I was floating on my back . . . I thought about the waves that had knocked me over on other days, about those few seconds each time when I would lose my bearings, let the sea shake me up and down while waiting confidently to float back up to the surface. I let it do the same thing now. I wasn't expecting anything. Something was slipping away.

"What the hell are you doing?"

A hand grabbed me. Luce pulled me up until I was standing, then dragged me forcibly back with her.

"I can't believe you're swimming now! Where were you? I called you so many times!"

She led me to the dune; not to where the others were but to the side, where there was a surf hut built on stilts. A wave swept away her sarong. She kept going in her swimsuit. She climbed the steps, felt around on the roof, found the key, and let us in. Then she closed the door behind us.

A little light and wind sneaked between the wooden slats. The hut smelled of sand and damp towels. Outside, the water kept rising. It caressed the stilts. The hut was tiny, like a boat in the night. I heard Luce breathing, very close. She smelled of alcohol. I probably did, too. She came closer. I stood leaning against the wall, waiting for her to do something.

"The campsite's going to be flooded. It's happened before, three years ago. It destroyed everything, it was horrible. There was a storm, too, with massive hailstones that smashed cars and hurt people, but I was happy. At least it changed things. I'm sick of this campsite. It's always the same. I know it all by heart. I don't like the campers. They all look the same . . . like the Landes, with all its stupid pine trees."

She came even closer. "I lost my sarong . . . Why did you mention Oscar before? I don't care about Oscar . . . He went crazy yesterday."

She was mixing everything up. Her hand touched mine and everything became mixed up for me, too: the alcohol, the hut surrounded by water, the bottles and bodies floating outside, Luce, sad and drunk and sweetly reassuring amid all this wreckage. I didn't know her. I had spent a long day with her, but I didn't know her, except for her voice, her pale skin, her dry lips. She kissed me. And then it happened. There was nothing violent about it. It was like tired music. The sensation wasn't really disorienting; it was pretty much like I'd imagined. It wasn't a liberation, either: I came, and the world stayed the same. Oscar and the waves continued outside. But something pleasant spread through my body, and I think through hers, too. She held me in her arms. I thought that I was in love with her and that it was the best thing that had happened to me in a long time. She fell asleep.

I woke up. The wind and the waves had died down. I'd been sleeping next to Luce on a pile of towels. Her arm was under my neck and our heads were touching. I carefully detached myself from her and left the hut. Outside, everything was calm. The sky was already tinged with pink. The sea had retreated, but during the night, the water had overflowed the dune and reached the campsite. It had left behind an altered beach. I didn't recognize it anymore. The bumps and the hollows had all switched places. A large part of the dune had collapsed. I took a few steps on the soaked sand, which was littered with trash from the party. After dawn, it would all be cleaned up. I had to find Oscar before then. But I was cold. Winter would reach this place. All that trouble, just for this. I went to find Luce and nestled against her. There were still a few hours of sleep left.

◆

MORNING CREPT THROUGH the slats. Luce took up a lot of space when she slept. She was sweating. The breath from her half-open mouth smelled sour. She moved in her sleep, forcing me to the edge of the towels as if they were a bed. She kept kicking and elbowing me, but I patiently put up with it. I could have stayed for hours in that position, bones aching but a smile on my face, my heart soothed by the knowledge that she was comfortable. Sometimes I wanted to kiss her shoulder, but I didn't dare disturb her. I watched her, waiting for her to wake up. I dreamed, eyes open . . . I met Luce and we are going to stay together. The bad years are behind me. The worst is just behind me. Oscar was swept away by the sea. Now he is drifting far from us, toward America. One day he will stop floating and he will sink to the bottom of the ocean, and that will be the end of it. We will live somewhere. I will atone for it, year by year. I will give back as much as I have ruined this August. I will pay my debt in silence. No one will come looking for us or make us do anything. We will have a gun to shoot pink bunnies.

Luce woke. She sat up, stretched, already impatient. "How are you, Leo? Did you sleep well?"

"Very well." I wanted to kiss her, but she started yawning.

She picked up her phone. "It's nine already!"

"Ah. What do you think we should do, Luce?"

"Your parents will be leaving at ten, won't they, like everyone else? You'd better hurry."

I felt less good now. Our condom—the one Louis had given me—was lying on the floor. I'd thought about throwing it away while Luce slept, but in the end I'd left it there. I'd thought we would look at it and laugh, complicit, that we would have sex again, perhaps, and that we'd then take a walk, hand in hand, to the main square, to eat brunch, pleasantly tired after our night. But she kept staring at her phone, smiling as she answered her messages.

She kissed me on the cheek and everything became wonderful again. I kissed her on the mouth, like a big thank-you.

"You should call your parents," she said.

"I lost my phone in the sea."

"Shit."

"Doesn't matter. There are worse things."

"Use mine." She gave it to me and lay down again. She wasn't trying to make me like her, that was obvious. Her neck folded and gave her a double chin. "I'm going to leave today, too. I don't think I'll ever come back to this campsite. In September, I start university, in Bordeaux. I'll try to spend my summers there."

How many miles were there between Bordeaux and Lorient? Probably not many, compared to the distance between other cities or countries. I googled it to check, covering the screen with my hand to shade it from the sunlight, even though there wasn't any; I'd used this same trick every time I'd pretended to send messages on the beach at night, so I wouldn't have to dance. No one had realized.

"So are you calling them or what?"

"Yeah, yeah . . ."

For a moment I imagined my phone in the depths of the sea, with all the missed calls from my mother. Then I looked at Luce and I couldn't hold it back any longer. "And *after*?" I asked, looking deep into her eyes for the first time.

"What, after?"

"After . . . will I see you again?"

She looked surprised. "We live a long way apart."

"Three hundred and twenty-one miles."

She smiled and looked at me kindly—that was all: kindly—and I felt something pinch my heart.

"I'll add you on Facebook. Leonard what?"

"I'm not on Facebook."

"Well, sign up."

I nodded several times.

"I'm sorry . . . Vacation's not like the rest of the year, you know what I mean?"

"I know what you mean."

"But I do like you, Leo."

"I like you, too, Luce."

She kissed me on the cheek and held me in her arms. I cried a bit and then it passed.

◆

"WILL THE PARENTS of the little girl paddling in the puddle opposite the barbecues please come and fetch her?"

It was gray, almost cold. Everything was sad and slow this Sunday. The ground was soaked, muddy, covered with puddles and little streams. The campers dug channels and hung out their wet clothes under the vanished sun. It was like a battlefield. Tubes of sunscreen and inflatable mattresses lay abandoned on the ground. Only the children kept riding bikes and shouting, because they were on vacation, and that was even sadder. It felt like fall, like the morning after the night before. I wanted to leave. Oscar was still sticking to my skin, damp and cold like seaweed, rotting foully somewhere. I couldn't remember his eyes.

Luce walked with me toward my tent. Both of us were silent. Bubble suddenly ran in front of us, like a happy escapee.

My father sprinted after him. "Come here, you little bastard!" He managed to grab the leash but fell face-first into a puddle. When he stood up, he glared at Bubble, then he noticed us. I realized that Luce had been holding my hand, because she let go of it just then.

"Hello," said my father.

"Hello," she replied.

He blushed. The blood rushed to his head. Even his ears turned red. He let go of Bubble's leash. The dog tried to run off again, but my mother appeared in time to stop him. "Hello."

"Hello, madame."

"We were looking for you," she told me.

I nodded.

"So . . . how are you?" my father asked, opening his arms wide and laughing nervously.

"Very well, thanks, and you?"

"Yes, yes, very well. Although it's always a bit sad when you have to leave."

"We'll be back next summer," my mother added.

"You should go to Bordeaux instead. It's pretty there."

"That's true. Bordeaux is very pretty . . ."

Bubble looked at the four of us as if we were stupid. Luce turned to me. "I'll be going, then. Goodbye, Leo."

"Goodbye . . ."

She kissed me without warning. My parents looked shocked and suddenly had lots of things to do with Bubble. Luce smiled at me. I thought she looked happy and sad at the same time, and she was even more fantastic like that. I sensed that I was looking at her for the last time. I wanted to talk to her more, but she was already leaving. When she had gone, my parents finally dared look at me again. They were shy and proud in a way I had never seen before. In that moment, I loved them.

"Are we leaving now?"

"Yes," said my father, starting to move. He added in English: "Yes, yes, yes, go."

◆

THEY HAD ALREADY folded up the tents. It was time to leave. The empty camping spot looked strangely insignificant. Just a square of dried grass. Somewhere here, I had spent fifteen nights. Fifteen times I had gotten up while the others were sleeping and walked blindly over to the hedge to take a piss, then tossed my tissue full of semen into the trash bin before going back to my tent. Nothing remained of all that. By the next day, another family might have taken our place and started their own vacation. Camping spot number 330. Happiness guaranteed for only twenty euros a night. Satisfying customers for decades, and for centuries to come. We strapped the bicycles to the back of the car and got in. We drove along the paths slowly, careful not to run over a child. My seat was too upright because of the luggage behind it. Bubble lay in his basket looking disappointed. Alma and Adrien were sad, too. They would soon be going back to school. Near the restrooms, we saw the pink bunny, although he wasn't really pink anymore: the filth had turned his fur brown. He was carrying a crate of empty beer bottles. He'd taken off his bunny head. Underneath was a man in his thirties, very tired-looking. The big grin drawn on his bunny face continued smiling at us from his back, where it hung like a severed head.

My parents were as silent as churchgoers before their suddenly grown-up son, happy and sad after his first summer of love. We drove through the main square. There were several policemen there. I closed my eyes. But my father parked close to the reception building. "I'm going to pay."

He got out. We waited for him. No one said a word.

I was frightened. For the first time, maybe, I felt that raw fear of being caught, without any other anxieties getting in the way. My pulse throbbed loud in my ears. I thought about airports and customs officers. Inside, my father was talking. It went on too long.

"Actually, Leo," said Adrien, without looking up from his phone, "you know your friend Louis? Well, something weird happened to him."

"What do you mean?"

"Some of the guys saw him on the beach very early this morning. Apparently he didn't look too good. He went swimming in the sea naked. He was floating facedown in the water. Which is okay, except he stayed like that too long. I mean, *way* too long . . ."

"What's all this about?" my mother asked, turning around. She gave me a questioning look, as if I knew the answer.

"In the end," Adrien went on, "a lifeguard went in and brought him out of the water. He's okay, don't worry. But it's a bit weird, all the same."

I nodded and looked outside. I touched the door handle.

"Leonard? Do you want to get out? Do you want to go and see your friend before we leave?"

"No, it's okay."

My father returned. "All right! So, time to say goodbye to the Landes."

"Daddy, why are there policemen here?"

"Because of the flood. Are you going to say goodbye to the Landes?"

"It's not because of that," Adrien corrected him. "It's because some guy disappeared."

"Oh, really?"

"Well, yeah."

"How do you know things like that?" Alma asked.

"Because I'm smart."

My mother fell silent. I kept my eyes on her.

"So . . . are you going to say goodbye to the Landes?" repeated my father, who didn't really care about all the other stuff.

"Goodbye, the Landes!"

He set off. We drove through the gates. As we turned onto the main road, I twisted my neck to get one last look at the campsite, and I thought I saw Claire in the main square. But then the luggage obstructed my view and the campsite disappeared.

◆

ALMA WAS ALREADY asleep. Adrien was texting his friends. The pines flashed past endlessly. We would have to drive for a long time before we stopped seeing them. I stared at them so I wouldn't have to see anything else. It was difficult. Gradually, in the gaps between them, I glimpsed other images: Luce was searching the beach for her lost sarong; she found it in the tall grass, near Oscar's damp, dirty body, which lay like a shipwreck victim washed ashore.

I sensed that my mother was still watching me in the

rearview mirror. That same look. I met her eyes. Maybe that was when she knew the truth for sure. I opened my mouth. I thought she was going to tell me not to say anything, to guard the secret deep inside me, but she didn't do anything; she just kept looking at me with her sad eyes. They were blue, her eyes. I'd never really noticed that before.

"Dad, I forgot something. Can we turn back?"

"Of course."

"Ugh, what a pain!" Adrien moaned.

"It's only six miles. We'll be there before you know it!"

◆

"HERE IS FINE," I said, just outside the campsite gates.

I didn't want them to come with me. My father parked on the roadside and put on his flashers. It wouldn't take long. I got out and walked to the reception building. The police car wasn't there anymore. Claire wasn't there, either. All was calm. Maybe they'd found Oscar somewhere on the beach. For a moment I wanted to go there, to see. But I was too tired. I needed to find a policeman, a stranger, a man well acquainted with death. I'd tell him everything and then it would be over.

The woman at the reception desk was busy with paperwork. She didn't see me as I sneaked into a corridor. I'd never been here before. It didn't look like a vacation place. In a room with an open door, I found my policeman. He was eating grated carrots straight from the plastic packaging.

"Excuse me. I'd like to talk to you."

"Okay, go ahead."

I closed the door and sat facing him. He looked surprised. He ate a few more mouthfuls and then he stopped. He waited for me to speak.

"Oscar died on Friday night. I don't know his surname, but he's the one who disappeared. I killed him."

He stared at me. "Don't move."

He was about to stand up, but just then some music came on and he froze. *This is the rhythm of the night . . .* His phone was ringing. He blushed and started rummaging around in his pockets, in his jacket, his bag. *This is the rhythm of the night . . .*

He doesn't find it. The phone keeps ringing. A cool breeze blows through the window—or maybe it's the ventilation system? The heatwave is over. The campsite is silent, as if everyone has already gone home. I don't know where Luce is. Outside, a broken vending machine beeps at regular intervals. *This is the rhythm of my life . . .* The music keeps trying to make me dance.

AUTHOR

VICTOR JESTIN is a twenty-six-year-old writer and screen-writer who grew up in northwestern France and now lives in Paris. *Heatwave* is his debut novel. Originally published by Flammarion under the title *La chaleur*, it won the Prix Femina des Lycéens and was nominated for the Prix Médicis and Prix Renaudot.

TRANSLATOR

SAM TAYLOR grew up in England, spent a decade in France, and now lives in the United States. He is the author of four novels and the award-winning translator of more than sixty books from the French, including Laurent Binet's *HHhH*, Leïla Slimani's *The Perfect Nanny*, and Maylis de Kerangal's *The Heart*.